WHAT YOU MADE ME

A week ago Philippa's life had been
relatively uncomplicated. But that was
before Scott Garson had strode back
into it, wanting revenge for what he
thought she had done to him eleven
years ago. . . .

Books you will enjoy
by PENNY JORDAN

WANTING

Heather might be a beautiful and successful model, but she was far from being the hardboiled, mercenary type a model is all too often assumed to be. So what right had Race Williams to treat her as if she was like that? And what on earth was she doing falling in love with him?

THE DARKER SIDE OF DESIRE

Saving the life of Sheikh Ahmed's young orphaned nephew had been a frightening and shocking experience for Claire Miles, and then the Sheikh had proposed that she should go to the Middle East and look after the boy. But there was one condition—to safeguard Saud's life, she would have to masquerade as his mother, with the arrogant and contemptuous Raoul D'Albro as the father!

RULES OF THE GAME

All her life Vanessa had accepted the fact that she was second rate compared to her stunning cousin Nadia; and she had harboured no resentment at being pushed into the background while Nadia's success as a model flourished. But that was until Jay Courtland mistook *her* for Nadia. . . .

CAMPAIGN FOR LOVING

Why had Blake Templeton decided to re-enter Jaime's life? Could it have anything to do with the attacks on her about the sale of the Abbey? But surely he would not endanger the life of his wife and daughter? Would he?

WHAT YOU MADE ME

BY

PENNY JORDAN

MILLS & BOON LIMITED
15–16 BROOK'S MEWS
LONDON W1A 1DR

First published in Great Britain 1984 by Mills & Boon Limited

© Penny Jordan 1984

Australian copyright 1984
Philippine copyright 1985
This edition 1985

ISBN 0 263 74903 7

Set in Monophoto Times 11 on 11½ pt.
01–0185 – 50611

Made and printed in Great Britain by Richard Clay (The Chaucer Press) Ltd, Bungay, Suffolk

CHAPTER ONE

WITH a thankful sigh Philippa sank back on her heels, surveying the stacked boxes and paper sacks, quickly stifling an unanticipated stab of pain as she looked at what was after all the accumulation of sixty odd years of living. How little she had really known about her aunt, and all that was left of her now was the faded photograph album Philippa had decided to keep. She hadn't wanted to come back to Garston, but she had been Jane Cromwell's only living relative.

Getting to her feet and dusting down her jeans she bent to pick up one of Simon's motorbike magazines. Her ten-year-old son was motorbike mad at the moment. Even from being quite small he had shown a decidedly mechanical turn of mind. At the moment it was fixed with equal concentration on motorbikes and computers.

Thinking of Simon made her glance at her watch and frown. It was gone five and she had told him to be back at four. She planned for them to have an early meal and then leave to go back to London. Where on earth was he? They had only been in Garston for a week but it was long enough for Simon, with his outgoing extrovert nature, to make friends. Several of them had called for him this morning. Unlike herself Simon made friends easily. There must still be people living in the village who re-

membered her, but apart from the vicar no one
had come to call.

Of course her aunt had always kept herself very
much to herself. Living as she did in what was
virtually a 'grace and favour' house on the
Garston estate, her isolation from the rest of the
village had tended to set her apart from the
villagers, just as it had set Philippa apart during
those years when she lived with her aunt. It
couldn't have been easy for her, Philippa now
recognised, to accept the responsibility of a
fourteen-year-old girl, still shocked by the sudden
death of her parents, and inclined to be rebellious
and withdrawn because of it. Her father, Jane
Cromwell's cousin, had been a diplomat, and he
and her mother had been killed during a terrorist
raid whilst Philippa was at school in England.

Their death had brought many changes to
Philippa's life, not the least of which was the
discovery that there was no longer enough money
for her to continue at the exclusive girls' school her
parents had sent her to. Her father's salary had
been generous but it had died with him, leaving
only the proceeds of two small insurance policies.
Her aunt had been a teacher and during the last
ten years of her career had had only one pupil—
Edward Garston, because of which she had been
gifted a lifetime's occupation of the small cottage
which became home to Philippa, and which stood
just within the boundary of the Garston family's
estate. Once they had owned vast acres of
Yorkshire, including the village named after the
family, but gradually over the years their land had
been eroded away with their wealth until all that

was left was the house itself, the parkland it stood in and the home farm. And then further tragedy had struck. Edward Garston had been killed in a car accident and his inheritance passed to a cousin, Scott.

Philippa could remember the day Scott and his mother arrived at Garston quite vividly. Scott's father had been the second son, the black sheep of the family and there was gossip in the village that his grandfather had sworn he would rather see the house and the estate pass to a stranger than go to his son's child. Scott had been twenty to her fourteen when he first came to live at Garston. Away at Oxford most of the time, Philippa could remember catching brief glimpses of him during the holidays, when invariably he arrived riding a large and noisy motorbike, his arrival always increasing his grandfather's already irascible temper. Jeffrey Garston was a proud, and Philippa had sometimes thought, very lonely old man, very bitter in his resentment of Edward's death at eighteen and of the cousin who had taken his place. Edward had been reputed to be brilliant and it was no secret in the area that Jeffrey Gaston had looked to his grandson to somehow recoup the family losses and restore Garston Hall to what it had once been. The Garston family fortune had been founded on coal and railways during the Victorian era, but now they were reduced to living on a rapidly dwindling income.

After what she had heard about the family Philippa had been rather surprised that Jeffrey Garston allowed his daughter-in-law and grandson to come and live with him, but he had done so and

moreover seemed to be training Scott to take over
what was left of the estate, because Philippa often
saw him in the holidays working at the farm, or
supervising the shoots which still took place in the
autumn, when large parties of businessmen would
descend on the Hall, and the narrow road that led
past the cottage to it would be busy with large,
expensive cars.

Where was Scott now? Philippa had only had
one letter from her aunt after she left and that had
simply told her that Jeffrey Garston had died and
that Scott had shut up the house and left the area.
That alone had surprised her. Scott had been
almost obsessed by his plans to make the estate a
viable commercial enterprise once more, and to
restore his home to what it had once been. She had
replied to her aunt's letter, telling her about
Simon's birth, but there had been no further
correspondence between them. A niece who bore
an illegitimate child had been so far outside Jane
Cromwell's own rigid moral code that there was
no question that there would ever be forgiveness
or acceptance, and certainly never a welcome in
her home for either Philippa or Simon. How
dramatic and terrifying it had all seemed eleven
years ago!

Philippa suppressed a faint sigh. Who would
have dreamed then that now women would choose
to bear their children alone without the support of
the child's father? Simon's lack of a father didn't
even cause so much as a faintly raised eyebrow
these days. Her own single-parent status was so
commonplace that more than half of Simon's
friends at his London school also lived with only

one of their parents. Eleven years ago when she discovered she was pregnant she had been terror-struck.

She grimaced as she caught a glimpse of herself in the mirror hanging on the wall. How very young and naive she had been. Seventeen and as green as grass. Well, she had learned, and now at twenty-eight, she knew without false modesty that she was an intelligent and even shrewd woman, who had learned about life the hard way.

What she failed to recognise in her own reflection was the vulnerability of her softly curved mouth; the shadows that darkened her grey eyes, the hint of pain that still lingered beneath the cool outer shell of reserve in which she cloaked her true feelings.

Her hair had been short when she left Garston. Her aunt had insisted that it was tidier that way. Now she wore it up in a nest chignon in keeping with her image as the efficient secretary to Sir Nigel Barnes, the Chairman of Merrit Plastics, but once released from its imprisonment it curled halfway down her back in honey-gold waves, silky soft and so directly in contrast to Simon's straight coal-black hair that people often did a double take when they were introduced as mother and son. Like his hair, Simon had inherited his height and breadth of shoulder from his father. At ten he looked closer to thirteen and was maturing quickly, too quickly, Philippa acknowledged, subduing the faint feeling of dismay she always felt when she contrasted Simon's upbringing with her own. Children were not allowed to remain naive for very long at the large London school Simon attended; sometimes she felt he was growing up too fast.

She sighed, and returned her attention to her appearance, pulling a wry face. Dressed in a pair of shabby jeans which had shrunk and were now barely decent, an old t-shirt which showed only too clearly that she had kept the slender figure she had had before Simon's birth, her hair tied back in a ponytail, wisps escaping to frame her face, she looked more like Simon's sister than his mother. Add to that, the fact that he was already two inches above her small five foot four, and their true relationship seemed even more ridiculous.

Thinking of her son, where was he? She glanced at her watch again. If he had one fault it was that when it came to time Simon was something of a dreamer. Once involved in some task time no longer seemed to matter to him. That he was extremely clever had been emphasised to her the last time she had visited his school. His headmaster considered him very gifted, and he had also pointed out rather wryly that it was unfortunate that in the modern secondary school of the type he would probably attend in London, he might not receive the individual tuition needed to make the most of his special gifts. The fact was that Simon, although brilliantly clever with his hands, with anything mechanical or mathematical, had, when it came to English and related subjects, something of a mental block, and as his headmaster had pointed out to Philippa, if Simon was to realise his full potential he would need to work hard to bring his English up to standard.

'Without at least an "O" level in it, he will never

make it to university,' he had told Philippa
frankly, adding 'Private tuition would be the thing,
but it would be very expensive. Another alternative
would be a smaller, country school where they
have more time to concentrate on individual
subjects.'

Both were out of the question. Her salary was a
good one, but living in London was expensive, too
expensive for her to be able to afford private
tuition, unless of course she could get an evening
job, but that meant leaving Simon on his own. As
it was she felt bitterly conscious of the fact that she
was at best a 'part-time mother' but what
alternative did she have? She was both mother and
father to Simon. She had to go out to work.

She heard a sound outside, a car coming
towards the cottage, and frowned. The lane the
cottage was on was the back road leading to the
Hall but was, according to the Vicar, not in use
any more, the company which had made Garston
Hall its headquarters using the main entrance. The
discovery that Garston Hall had been taken over
by Computex, a highly successful computer
company, had rather surprised her. For one thing
Garston was so remote, fifty miles from York,
right in the middle of the Yorkshire Dales. That
meant that Scott must have sold it, but then she
had known he would have to when he refused to
marry Mary Tatlow. His grandfather had been
desperately keen for him to marry her. Her father
was a millionaire and once married to her Scott
could have looked to his new father-in-law to
provide the money to restore Garston. But Scott
had apparently refused to comply with his

grandfather's wishes. That had been something else her aunt had written in her last letter.

The sound of the car engine was getting louder. Philippa leaned out of the small casement window, frowning as she saw the enormous gleaming Rolls pushing its way down the overgrown lane, her frown deepening when she saw the huge dent and scraped paint on the front wing. The damage had obviously been caused recently and, to judge from the extent of it, would be horrendously expensive to repair. But then perhaps to a man who could afford to buy such a car the cost of a repair which she judged would probably buy her a very nice small car, meant nothing. The car stopped outside the cottage. The rear door opened and Philippa saw Simon getting out.

She hurried downstairs, wondering how on earth her son had managed to cadge a ride in the car, torn between amusement at his enterprise and maternal anger that he should have ignored all her warnings to him on the subject of strange cars and potentially even stranger men.

The first thing that struck her as she opened the door was that Simon looked extremely pale; the second was that her normally voluble son was suspiciously quiet. A car door slammed and her eyes tracked automatically to the man walking down the narrow weed-infested path, her heart doing a double somersault before lurching to a spectacular standstill. 'Scott!'

'So he *is* your son.' He had ignored her whispered acknowledgement of him and stood behind Simon, dwarfing her tall, gangly son. As Philippa knew from experience Scott would have to duck his head a good six inches to pass under the low lintel to the cottage. Ten years had effected various changes in him but the one she registered first was the total lack of pleasure or warmth in his eyes as they rested on her, their deep blue depths which she remembered as warm and sunny, freezing her with the dislike he made no effort to conceal.

Eleven years since she had last seen him. He had been twenty-three, almost twenty-four, now he would be thirty-five. He was wearing an expensively tailored suit very much in keeping with the Rolls parked outside the cottage, but totally out of keeping with the Scott she remembered who had worn faded, ancient jeans, whose hair had brushed his shirt collars untidily, whose face had been open, always brimming with humour, his eyes always darkening with teasing laughter.

She shivered suddenly despite the warmth of the May sun. It was like standing in the path of a blast of arctic weather looking into his eyes. His face hadn't changed though really, merely settled. He had always been very physically attractive, although time had added a certain degree of muscled hardness to the body she remembered as thinner, more boyish, and his face, the face that betrayed the hint of Spanish blood on his mother's side of the family, was more arrogant, the grooves running from nose to mouth more defined. As a young man growing to maturity he had been devastatingly attractive and yet in many ways unaware of his appeal for her sex.

He was still every bit as physically compelling, perhaps even more so, but now there was a look in his eyes that told her he knew exactly what effect he had on her sex, and Philippa withdrew from the sexual explicitness it with a distasteful grimace she only realised he had witnessed when she saw the anger flare in his eyes.

So that at least had not changed. He still possessed a temper ... the temper which had perhaps led him to defy his grandfather and refuse the marriage the old man had planned for him?

'Simon, where have you been?' Philippa asked her son, turning her attention to him and hoping that Scott wouldn't notice the hot colour painting her skin. 'You know I wanted to leave early.' If his hair and his bone structure were his father's it was from her that Simon had inherited his grey eyes and the shape of his face. His mannerisms were hers as well, and she watched him scuffing his toes, his expression woebegone and guilty. Her mind too bemused with Scott's wholly unexpected arrival to pay more than fleeting attention to Simon, she was startled when Scott said grimly, 'I'll tell you where he's been. Trespassing on Computex land; riding a motorcycle for which I imagine I am correct in saying he has no licence. A motorbike which, moreover,' he continued inexorably, 'he crashed into my car.'

In a daze Philippa looked out of the window at the huge dent in the gleaming car, her glance going from that to her son's milk-white face. Her appalled 'Oh, Simon, how could you ...' drawing a gruff, 'It was an accident honest, Mum. ... It was broken and I'd been helping to mend it and then Tommy Hargreaves said I could have a go on it for helping them . . . I didn't know it was private land.'

He shot a scared glance at Scott and Philippa's heart went out to him. Poor Simon, what on earth had Scott been saying to him to make him look so terrified? And that dent in the car? Surely that hadn't been caused simply by Simon? 'Tommy told me they always used it for racing on . . . I told him I didn't have a licence but he said it wouldn't matter. And then. . . .

'. . . and then I was on my way to the home farm to check on something with my Manager when this young fool came riding out of the trees and nearly ran straight into me. If I hadn't swerved to avoid him, I doubt he'd be here in one piece now,' Scott concluded grimly, whilst several facts hit Philippa at the same time. 'On my way to the home farm,' Scott had said, which must mean he was back living at Garston . . . And 'swerved to avoid Simon', which meant that Simon hadn't run into him after all!

She went up to her son, hugging him tightly and for once Simon didn't squirm away. For all his size he was very much her little boy, his eyes dark and afraid. 'It was an accident, Mum,' he said desperately. 'I tried to explain, but Mr . . . Mr. . . .'

'Garston,' Scott supplied sardonically, glancing coldly at Philippa. 'I see you haven't told him much about that part of your life which preceded his birth, Philippa . . . I wonder why?'

'You said you swerved to avoid Simon, which means he didn't do the damage to your car,' Philippa interrupted, without answering.

'Not physically perhaps,' Scott agreed, 'but I

don't doubt that any court would lay the blame at
his feet, as well as taking a pretty dim view of the
fact that he was riding the machine without the
benefit of a licence and trespassing on private
land. It's going to cost several thousand pounds to
put the damage right.'

Philippa's mouth went dry. Several thousand
pounds, and how Scott would delight in making
her pay, in extracting every last penny. He had
sworn vengeance on her, eleven years ago, and she
had laughed it aside, never dreaming that the
future might hold this. Was he remembering that
hot summer afternoon, when she told him she was
leaving?

She looked at him and knew that he was. Once she
had thought she loved him and once too he had
thought he loved her, but it had all been a long time
ago, an adolescent romance for her, a summer affair
for him, both of them poised on the brink of other
things with a summer to spare, but she had hurt his
pride when she threw his love back in his face, and it
showed in his eyes that he had not forgiven her.

'Scott. . . .' She took a step towards him and saw
his instant recoil and knew that the plea which had
been on her lips to let the past lie could not be
uttered. He wanted it to remain alive; he wanted to
punish her, and could she really blame him? She
had told him she loved him and then she had gone
to tell him that she had made a mistake and that
she loved someone else. He had every right to
resent, perhaps even hate her, whilst she. . . .

'Mum. . . .' She came out of her thoughts to find
Simon watching her. Sometimes he saw too much
and worried her with his maturity.

'Go upstairs, Simon,' she told him. 'You still haven't packed, and I want to leave as soon as possible.'

When he had gone she faced Scott, neither asking him to come in or preventing him from doing so. This house which had been her aunt's belonged to the estate and would revert to it with her death, and Scott had every right to walk into it with or without her permission.

'I'm sorry about your car.' She took a deep breath. 'Simon doesn't tell lies, and we haven't been here long enough for him to know that the estate is private. . . .'

'What are you trying to say? That he was misled? He's how old? Twelve? Thirteen?'

'Ten.' Red flags of colour sprang into her cheeks. Scott knew exactly how old Simon was, damn him.

'He looks much older. Our magistrates are rather old-fashioned around here. They take a dim view of damage to private property. As well as the damage to the car there'll probably be a hefty fine to pay, always supposing of course that they accept this as a first offence.'

First offence! Philippa's body went cold. 'It was an accident,' she said desperately. 'You. . . .'

'Can you prove that? I could claim that it was malicious damage. I thought you were never going to come back here, Philippa. I thought your lover was going to take you away . . . somewhere glamorous. . . . The south of France I believe you said. . . . How long did it take him to realise what a cheat you were? Not long, to judge from the speed with which he left you. He was back at

Woolverton by Christmas and married the following spring to Mary Tatlow. Your aunt was very disappointed in you, Philippa. She did say that she never wanted to see you again if I remember correctly.'

'I was her only relative, when she died I. . . .'

'Came back out of a sense of loyalty to her, is that what you're trying to say?' he jeered, anger splintering through the cold façade he had adopted towards her. 'Don't try to make me believe that. I know exactly how much your loyalty is worth. . . .'

'Scott, I. . . .'

'You what? Made a mistake? When did you discover that? When Geoff refused to marry you despite the fact that you were carrying his bastard child? No wonder you left so quickly. It was quite a nine-day wonder, I can tell you, especially as he left at the same time. "There's someone else," you told me in that cool, butter wouldn't melt voice. "I can't marry you, Scott . . . I love someone else . . ." and then you left . . . cool as the proverbial cucumber . . . *after* you told me you were carrying his child. Have you any idea what you did to me? *Have you?*' he demanded savagely . . . 'I'd defied my grandfather for you. I was even prepared to leave Garston . . . to give up everything for you. But I wasn't enough for you, was I? As soon as you found out that my grandfather would disinherit me if we married, you dropped me flat and took up with Geoff Rivers. Did you tell him that I was the one who had your virginity or didn't he care? He ran out on you in the end though, didn't he, Philippa? He left you, carrying his child

. . . . alone . . . and you'll never know just how much pleasure knowing that gave me. . . .'

'I think I can guess.' She sounded calm but she had gone paper white. The force of his anger pounded against her in waves, battering against her defences, forcing her to remember things she would rather forget; that final scene with him; the pain that followed. . . .

'Yes, you always were quite quick on the uptake. . . . So quick that I still find it hard to understand why you ever let me make love to you in the first place. If you'd still been a virgin you might have got more out of Geoff than a bastard child . . . as it was, you'd have been hard put to prove which of us was the father.'

'I don't want to talk about it.' She could feel hysteria building up inside her, an aching, panicky pain she remembered from long ago and which she had kept deliberately at bay in the years that followed.

'Then what do you want to talk about? How you're going to pay for the repairs to my car? *My* car, Philippa, not Computex's. . . . Oh yes, Computex belongs to me. I made good after all you see. . . . You should have stuck with me; despite being disinherited I made it after all. My godfather helped me, and with that and a large slice of good luck I managed to hold on to Garston. Just think if you hadn't run out on me you'd be mistress of us both now . . . Garston and me . . . I always did wonder which of us meant the most to you. . . .'

'Neither.'

'No, of course not. I was forgetting about

Geoff. How easily you deceived me. . . . Did you enjoy it, you bitch, letting me think you loved me when all the time . . .?'

'Scott . . . about your car.' She wet her lips nerving herself for the admission she had to make. 'I'm afraid that I . . . I just don't have that sort of money. . . .'

'How very unfortunate for you. . . . So . . . what do you suggest I do? Simply wipe it off—put it down to "experience"?' He shook his head, baring his teeth slightly in a vulpine grimace. 'You've already cost me far too much under that heading. 'Oh, no,' he said softly, 'this time I'm going to do some recouping. You made a laughing stock out of me eleven years ago, Philippa, and now it's my turn to turn the screw a little.'

'Simon! You can't punish him because. . . .'

'Who said anything about punishing the boy? It's you I want to punish, Philippa. You who's going to pay, and if you can't pay in cash then you're going to have to pay in kind, as they say.'

A kind of numb terror seemed to hold her in its grip, a complete inability to reason logically, a primeval dread that made it impossible for her to shake off the spell Scott's voice was weaving round her. All she knew was that Scott had the power to hurt her son, and that somehow she must stop him from doing so no matter what the cost to herself.

'Scott, please. . . .'

'Please what? Spare your son? Very well . . . but only at a price, Philippa.'

'What is it?'

'You work as a secretary in London 1 understand, for Merrit Plastics.'

Philippa nodded her head, perplexed both by his question and the fact that he knew so much about her.

'You will give your notice in and come and work for me here at Garston.'

'As your secretary?'

'That . . .' he paused and added significantly, 'and other things.' Blood stormed her face as he looked at her, assessing and stripping her, making his meaning all too plain.

'Never.'

The bitter denial reverberated between them, his eyes darkening, going cold and hard as he breathed softly, 'Think again, Philippa . . . I've ached for an opportunity like this, an opportunity to get even with you and humiliate you the way you humiliated me . . . and now that I've got it I won't let go easily. Either way you make a sacrifice. It's up to you whether it's you or your son. . . .'

'But I can't work for you and. . . .'

'Share my bed? Of course you can, isn't it what you did for Rivers? You were working for him when you started sleeping with him weren't you? A holiday job I believe you called it. I want your answer and I want it now, Philippa, otherwise I'm taking your son to the police to make a statement. I doubt they'll let him off leniently.'

'Scott, don't make me do this . . . I've got Simon to think of. I can't. . . .'

'You can and you will, and if the boy doesn't know what manner of woman his mother is by now, I suspect it's time he found out. Don't try to tell me that Geoff was the last man in your life. A woman like you who takes two lovers at a time could never. . . .'

He caught her hand as it arched towards his face, grasping her wrist painfully, making her cry out with the numbing agony that shot down her arm.

'Make your mind up, Philippa. Either you come to me and let me use you for whatever purpose I desire, or I take your son to the police. . . .'

What choice did she really have? Her very silence confirmed her submission, and as she looked up and saw the triumph glittering in Scott's eyes she recognised that either she had never really known him, or the man she had known was gone for ever. Was she to blame for that? Was she to blame for what Scott seemed to have become—a cold, hard stranger who talked so calmly of revenge, and making her pay, a man who seemed to have no room in his life for either pity or compassion? It seemed that Scott thought she was and she shivered, partly in pain, partly in fear, wondering how she could have miscalculated all those years ago.

She had been so sure that he would marry Mary; so sure that she had been doing the right thing. So sure . . . and so wrong. But it was too late to go back now, far far too late.

She looked into his face and the thought struck her that perhaps if she stayed she might be able to put right the past, to make Scott see that what she had done she had done not to hurt him but because she had thought it was right, not against him but for him, and it was to this tenuous hope that she clung as she said slowly, 'Very well, Scott

. . . if that's what you want we'll stay, but I'll have to find somewhere to stay . . . a school for Simon. . . .'

'What's the matter with the local grammar school, or isn't that good enough for Geoff's bastard? His son, his legitimate son should I say, is down for Harrow, so I'm told, but of course men don't lay out good money to send their bastards to public school, do they?' He turned towards the door, and then paused, looking back at her over his shoulder as he said coolly, 'Don't worry about finding somewhere to stay, you'll both be staying at the house with me. . . .' He saw the expression in her eyes and laughed softly. 'Yes, it will cause quite a stir in the village, won't it, but nothing to the stir we're going to cause . . . nothing to the stir you caused when you dropped me and went off with Geoff. You should have heard my grandfather crow after you'd gone.'

His eyes were bitter and Philippa sensed that Scott was looking back to that time when he first came to Garston and was very much an outsider, very much the unwanted grandson taking the place—usurping the place—of the favourite dead one, his grandfather bitterly resentful of him and taking no pains to conceal his resentment.

'I'll be back tomorrow to take you and the boy up to the house. Don't try running out on me, Philippa, I'll come running after you and I won't be in any mood to be generous.'

The sound of his car had died away completely before Simon came downstairs. Philippa gave him a shaky smile and he came over to her, putting his arm around her waist, so very like his father in the quiet seriousness of his gaze that her heart ached. She ruffled the dark hair. 'He's gone then?'

'Umm. . . .'

'And he doesn't know?'

Something in his tone alerted her, some inner voice urging her to tread carefully. 'Know what?'

Simon looked at her directly. 'That he's my father,' he said quietly. 'You didn't tell him that I'm his son? I saw it on my birth certificate,' he told her quickly, 'ages ago, but it never really clicked until we came here and everyone was Scott Garston this and Scott Garston that. . . .' Of course! He had spent far more time in the village than she had, but she had had no idea he knew that Scott was his father. 'Tell me about it,' he insisted.

She supposed she owed him that, and if they were going to stay here. . . . If? Did she have any choice? And why had she given in? Because of some crazy impulse that there were still happy endings; that the past could be wiped out; that Scott could be made to see. . . . What?

She sat down, too wrapped up in her own thoughts for a moment to answer Simon's questions. When she left Garston she had sworn that she would put Scott out of her mind, but had she ever done? Why, when she hadn't lacked the opportunities, had she never had a relationship with anyone else? Why had she reacted as she did the moment she saw him? Did she still love him? Did she even know what love was? Certainly not that ridiculous overwhelming emotion; that adolescent self-sacrifice she had felt at seventeen—that had been part hero worship and part adoration, but she wasn't indifferent to Scott, her senses told her that much, and she would like to wipe out the bitterness, the fierce resentment she saw in his eyes, and to replace it with what? Respect? Love? Who knew? To nurture resentment and anger as long as he had done a man would have to be very powerfully motivated; very powerfully. . . .

'Come on, Ma, give. I want the whole story,' Simon warned her.

'Okay then . . .' she glanced at her son, so like his father for all that Scott couldn't see it, and said teasingly, 'Once upon a time. . . .'

CHAPTER TWO

INCREDIBLY it had had a fairytale quality to it; two lonely young people who had found one another, who had come together, loving and giving without restraint, sharing their thoughts, talking, always talking. . . . At least that was how it had been at first. She had been in the garden, studying for her 'A' levels, Scott had been walking past, and instead of walking past had come in. They had started talking and discovered a mutual love of the Renaissance, and it had gone on from there. He had invited her up to the Hall, she remembered, to see some of the books in the library, including one which charted the history of the old Abbey which had stood where the Hall now stood and which had been a victim of Henry VIII's nefarious Reformation. And it had continued, companionship giving way to love so sweetly and naturally that it had seemed the most natural, the most beautiful thing in the world. She had never felt a moment's fear in Scott's presence; never a moment's dread, or apprehension.

The first time he kissed her she had given herself into his keeping absolutely. *Her* first kiss, but not his, but it had left both of them trembling and she, she remembered, had been the one who had reached out and touched him afterwards; the sun-burned skin of his throat and arms, the angles of his jaw, touching his skin wonderingly whilst he let her, his body held tightly under control. 'I love you'.

Which of them had said it first? She couldn't remember, only that the words seemed to dance round them in the lazy gold of a summer afternoon; that her body yearned for the touch of his; that their mutual loneliness intensified their love. And they were both lonely. She because of her aunt's strict upbringing, him because he was a newcomer to the village, an unwelcome intruder in his grandfather's life. His friends from university had gone and he was alone . . . they were both alone.

Even before they made love he had told her he wanted to marry her. And she had wanted to marry him and live with him at Garston.

Right from the start he had confided to her his love for Garston, the house which had become his by death. He knew and sympathised with his grandfather's views, but that didn't alter his own feelings for Garston. He worried about how he was going to keep it, where he would find the money to maintain and restore it, and it was with her that he shared his hopes and plans.

And then there had been his mother, Eve Garston, whom Philippa had liked on sight. Already even then severely disabled by arthritis, Eve had been wholly dependent on her irrascible father-in-law financially. Scott's father had been an engineer, and with his death the family had lost their source of income. Without the small allowance Jeffrey Garston paid them it would not have been possible for Scott to go to university, he would have had to take a job to support himself and his mother.

Carefully Philippa explained all this to her son, watching compassion and understanding add an odd maturity to his youthful features, yielding to a traitorous inner impulse to paint his father for him in knightly colours, because that was how she had remembered him. All through the years she had cherished her memories of Scott, refusing to tarnish them, hugging them to her for comfort in those times when she needed it so badly—when she first arrived in London, virtually penniless; when Simon had been born six months later at the home for unmarried mothers. Jobs had been easier to get in those days and with the help of the people who ran the Home she had learned shorthand and typing at college during her pregnancy, and then afterwards she had found a job, gradually progressing in her career, gradually improving the quality of their lifestyle. It had been a slow and painful progress, but nothing to compare with the pain of leaving Scott.

'Why didn't he marry you—was it because of me?' Pain and rejection mingled in the grey eyes so like her own.

'No.' Philippa reassured him quickly, 'No, it was nothing like that. Scott wanted to marry me before . . . before I was having you, and. . . ' she bit her lip, forcing herself to speak calmly, 'and if he'd known you were his nothing would have stopped him from marrying me . . . but I told him that someone else was your father.'

She saw the shock darkening Simon's eyes and rushed into an explanation. 'It was for his sake, Simon. His grandfather bitterly resented him and the fact that he would inherit Garston, but Scott loved it. . . .'

'More than he loved you?'

'Not more, just in a different way, and then there was his mother, Eve.' She sighed. 'She suffered from arthritis and needed an operation to help her to walk again. She would have had to wait years to have it done on the National Health but Scott's grandfather had promised to pay for her to have it done privately. He found out that Scott and I were in love and he sent for me.'

Her eyes darkened unwittingly as she remembered that day. The message had arrived just after breakfast, and her aunt had compressed her mouth angrily. She hadn't known anything about her relationship with Scott and had assumed that Philippa was being summoned for some other crime like riding her bike too close to the main gates. In many ways Jeffrey Garston was positively feudal, one of the conditions that went with Jane's tenancy of the cottage was that she and her niece used the narrow back road to and from their home; that they 'kept to their place'.

There had been no sign of Scott when Philippa was shown into the linenfold panelled library. Later she learned he had driven his mother into York to see a specialist, but at the time her nerves had tightened apprehensively when she realised she was alone with his grandfather. Jeffrey Garston had always unnerved her. Small and wiry he still had a full head of snow-white hair, and eyes the same deep sapphire as Scott's, although in Jeffrey Garston they were cold burning with the touch of ice—like Scott's had been last night, Philippa realised with a sudden start. He hadn't offered her a seat or done anything to make her feel less uncomfortable.

He knew about their affair, he had told her contemptuously, and she remembered how darkly she had flushed at the implications of his comment. The first time they had made love had been in Scott's bedroom. He had taken her up there quite innocently to show her the view. She had turned back from the window, dizzied by the panorama spread out in front of her, and Scott had caught her. After that events had run smoothly into one another until she couldn't remember who had made the first betraying movement, who had touched whom first, or how they had arrived at Scott's bed.

Afterwards he had been anxious and filled with self-anger for taking her virginity, but Philippa had gloried in his possession of her, giving herself willingly and glad of the sharp pang of pain which meant she was his and his alone. It was true that his response to her had rather overwhelmed her. He had always seemed so strong and sure and it was startling to discover that her touch could make him tremble, that his body could riot out of control; that his need for her could make his voice raw and hungry and that his body could over-rule his mind.

'Now you'll have to marry me,' he had told her in deep satisfaction, 'and your aunt will have to give her permission. . . .'

She smiled sadly, coming to with a start to realise that Simon was watching her curiously. 'Go on,' he pressed, 'what happened when Scott's grandfather sent for you?'

'He told me that he wanted Scott to marry the daughter of a friend of his,' Philppa told him calmly. 'This man was very rich and had promised that if Scott married his daughter he would give him enough money to restore and run Garston. Scott didn't know anything about it, but his grandfather knew how much he loved the house and believed that if I wasn't there to distract him he would soon turn to Mary.'

'But how did he make you agree? Why didn't you tell my father what he had said?'

Philippa sighed. How could she explain to Simon how she had felt, wanting Scott and yet knowing that if she married him she would be depriving him of his birthright; she would be saddling him with the double burden of a wife and an invalid mother. And then she hadn't known about Simon.

'Try to understand, Simon,' she begged her son. 'Your father would have married me, he wanted to even before ... we ... but he was in a difficult position. His mother was totally dependent on him, his grandfather was threatening to disinherit him which he could quite easily have done. I didn't realise then about you, and I felt that I just couldn't allow him to throw everything away because of me. . . .'

'If you had known about me would you have changed your mind?' Simon asked her gravely. Philippa sighed, reaching out and taking his hand and for once he did not withdraw. 'No. In fact. . . .' She might as well tell him the whole truth. 'Scott wouldn't believe me when I told him it was over between us, and then I found out about you. I was desperate, Simon, I knew if Scott ever guessed I was carrying his child he would insist on marrying me. He had just left university . . . he had no job, and I knew he wanted to study computer technology, so I . . . so I told him that there was someone else and that I was having this other man's child.'

Simon's face was as white as her own. In silence they stared at one another and for the first time Philippa reflected on what she had cost her son in her attempts to protect his father. Even now she could still remember that final scene—vividly. Scott had come to the cottage, furiously angry at her refusal to see or speak to him. 'Cut it out, Philippa,' he had stormed at her. 'I know damned well how you feel about me . . . I was your lover. . . .'

'That means nothing.' She had said the words more on impulse than anything else, totally unprepared for the way his face drained of blood, for the way he looked at her, his pride stripped to the bone, his love for her darkening his eyes with pain.

'Dear God, you can't mean that,' he had whispered, 'you don't know what you're saying.'

'Of course I do.' She had seen then what she must do, and had played her part with a recklessness born of sheer desperation. 'You haven't been my only lover, Scott,' she taunted. 'Just my first. . . .'

'You're lying. . . .'

'No.'

'Prove it to me.' His voice had been a whiplash of pain and agony, and she had had to close her eyes against her need to give in to tell him everything, knowing that if she did so he would leave Garston. 'All right ... I've been having an affair with someone, and I'm having his child.'

Dear God, even now she could feel the reverberations of her announcement; she could almost feel the quality of the deep silence that followed, Scott's bitter, 'Who?' throwing her off-guard so that she snatched the first name she could think of, Geoff Rivers; the local Lothario son of a wealthy businessman who streaked through the village at the wheel of his scarlet Ferrari.

'Him?' His face and voice had tortured her. 'Dear God, how could you ...?'

'Quite easily, actually.' She had tossed her head, wondering why he didn't know she was crying inside, wondering why he didn't come to her and say 'I know you're lying, you could never give yourself to anyone but me, and nothing matters but that we're together, nothing. ...'

But he didn't, he simply stood there and condemned her with his eyes watching her with such contempt that she had wanted to die. 'And to think I was prepared to defy my grandfather, to give up Garston for you.'

'We've both had a lucky escape, then, haven't we?' She had tossed her head again, aching inside with anguish but refusing to give in to it. 'I thought you were fun, Scott, but you're not. ...'

'Fun? Is that why you went to Rivers? Well go to him again and try telling him about his bastard, I'll bet he won't be much "fun" then.'

He had left then, and she had only waited until he had gone to give way to her tears. Later that

day an envelope had come to her from his
grandfather. When she opened it there had been
five hundred pounds in cash inside. She remembered the acute feeling of nausea which had
stormed over her even now. She had torn the notes
up and sent them back, and then she had packed
her clothes leaving only a brief note of explanation
for her aunt which simply told her that she was
pregnant. That had been the last contact she had
had with anyone from Garston until her aunt's
death.

'Did you really love each other?' Simon looked
pale and uncertain.

'Very much,' she assured her son. He might not
have the security of legitimacy, of knowing the
warmth and love of a real family, but at least she
would not rob him of the knowledge that he had
been conceived in love. 'That was why I left him,
Simon, because I loved him so much, and that is
why he was so angry with me when he came here,
because he loved me and he thought I had
betrayed him with another man.'

'But you didn't, and he didn't marry that Mary,'
Simon told her, adding, 'I know he didn't because
Rob Harrison told me that he wasn't married and
that he'd only just come back to live here. He was
talking about him you see and when he said his
name I recognised it, and I wanted to know
more. . . .'

Philippa's heart ached. Simon had known who
his father was and yet he had never talked to her
about him, just as she had never mentioned Scott
to him.

'Do you still love him?' She saw the hope

building up in Simon's eyes and shook her head, hating herself for what she must do. 'I don't think so, Simon. It was all a long time ago.'

'But he might still love you,' Simon pressed. 'He isn't married. If you told him about me?'

Poor Simon, how could she explain? 'He wouldn't believe me, Simon, he's changed. He hates me now.'

'But he wants us to stay here. I heard him say so.' Simon looked at her stubbornly.

'Not because he loves me. If anything he hates me. I hurt him very badly when I left, Simon,' she told him steadily, 'and when people hurt us we want to hurt them back, you know that.'

'If he wants to hurt you he couldn't have loved you all that much in the first place. . . .'

Unwittingly Simon had put his finger on the small ache that still lived inside her and which had grown to mammoth proportions whilst she listened to Scott's bitterly vitriolic comments. Had Scott ever really loved her as she had loved him or had he simply convinced himself that he had because she was there and they were both lonely?

What did it matter now? It was all in the past, and the gentle caring man she remembered no longer existed.

'If you hadn't ridden that bike illegally we wouldn't have to stay here,' Philippa pointed out dryly, 'What were you doing?'

'I managed to fix it and Tommy offered me a ride for doing it. He said that no one ever used that road, and that it was perfectly safe. They called me chicken when I refused.'

He shrugged thin boyish shoulders, narrow in

depth despite their width, the childish ribs clearly defined beneath his thin t-shirt. He grew so quickly, already out of the jeans and t-shirts she had bought only three months ago. He looked pale, too, compared with the village children, she had noticed, and she remembered what his headmaster had said about him doing better in a small school.

'I'd like to stay here.' He looked at her guilelessly, but Philippa wasn't deceived.

'We don't have much option,' she told him dryly.

'No, I wonder why he wants you to stay?'

So that he can humiliate me and make me suffer as he once did, Philippa could have told him, but she didn't want to burden Simon with her own dark thoughts. She could tell that he was fascinated by the subject of Scott and could she really blame him. The discovery of his father's existence was no doubt a heady experience, and she warned dampeningly, 'Don't get any silly ideas, Simon, and please promise me that you won't tell anyone that Scott is your father.' She saw his face and said gently, 'It's for your sake as much as mine.'

'Because you think he won't want me?'

'Something like that.' How could she explain again that she doubted that Scott would believe him. 'It's all in the past now and better forgotten.'

'But I'm not in the past. I'm here and he's my father.'

'Simon. . . .'

'Oh, it's all right, I won't say anything. I'm going to bed.'

He stamped upstairs, but not before she had seen the quick sheen of tears in his eyes. Dear God, if she stayed here what was it going to do to her son? But what option did she have? If she tried to leave she knew that Scott would have no compunction at all about carrying out his threat. There was no way she could afford to pay for the damage to his car, and she shuddered a little as she remembered Simon telling her how Scott had had to swerve into the tree to avoid hitting him. Simon was lucky that he wasn't lying in hospital right now, and she only hoped he appreciated that fact.

She was up early, sleep being impossible, and sat down to write some letters. Her flat she could easily sub-let, but for how long? She had no idea how long Scott intended to keep her here. At the back of her mind, only half acknowledged, lay the fact that Simon now knew who his father was and had made it clear to her that if it were possible he would like to form a relationship with him. She didn't pretend it was going to be easy—the chances were that if Scott did discover the truth and believe it he would still reject Simon, but did she have the right to deprive Simon of that one chance of getting close to his father? And who knew, in discovering the truth Scott might find a release from the burden of bitterness he obviously still carried around with him.

There was a telephone in the cottage, mercifully still connected, and she used it to phone her boss and explain that she wasn't coming back. As she had expected he was shocked and inclined to protest, but in the end gave way, knowing that she was right when she pointed out that there were at least half-a-dozen other girls in the firm who had the potential to take her place.

'Best secretary I've ever had,' he grumbled when she explained that she had decided to stay in Yorkshire. 'But if you've made up your mind——'

'Simon wants to stay and—I've been offered this job.'

'With Computex, you say? Umm, excellent firm, doing very well right now and they've managed to fight off two takeover bids very successfully. Who will you be working for did you say?'

Philippa hadn't, but she knew Sir Nigel well enough to know when he wasn't going to be put off. 'Scott Garston,' she told him.

'Umm. He's the Chairman and brain behind the company, isn't he? Think I met him once. Tall dark chap, sharp as a knife, but always looks unhappy. Shouldn't like to get on the wrong side of him, so I suppose I'd better let you go. . . . Don't want him making a takeover bid for Merrit Plastics.'

Philippa laughed dutifully, Sir Nigel was notorious for his shrewd business sense and she doubted that anyone would be foolhardy enough to dare to even think about taking over his precious company, much less Scott, who surely had enough on his plate with Computex. She was remembering more about the company now that the first shock of seeing him had died away. There had been a long report on them in the financial press recently, although it hadn't mentioned Scott by name.

Simon came downstairs just as she replaced the receiver. He looked tired and pale and avoided her eyes as he found a packet of cereal and poured some into his bowl.

'We're staying then,' he said, betraying that he had overheard her conversation, his voice telling her that she still wasn't wholly forgiven.

'It's what you wanted isn't it?' Philippa asked dryly. 'I'll have to ring your school . . . it's just as well it's half term at the moment. I'll have to go and see the headmaster here, see if there's a place for you.'

'Where will we live? Here?'

Philippa glanced round the cottage, her heart lifting. Could she persuade Scott to let them keep the cottage? Her spirits plummeted swiftly as she heard the sound of a car outside, not the Rolls this time but a bright red Ferrari. Her face burned as she watched Scott climb out of it and come towards the door.

'I see you do remember it,' he said coldly when she opened the door. 'Rivers owned one didn't he, far more impressive than the bike that was my only transport at the time—either that or grandfather's old Bentley. You should have stuck with me, Philippa.' He saw Simon sitting at the table and broke off to glance at him.

'Simon and I were just wondering if you'd allow us to stay in the cottage while I'm working for you?'

His mouth twisted and her heart sank as she saw the contempt darkening his eyes. 'What for?' He said it quietly so that Simon couldn't hear. 'So that you can entertain your lovers discreetly? No. I've already promised this place to someone else, and besides, I want you where I can see you

Philippa. I wonder what they'll say in the village when they know you're working for me?'

'Probably simply that I was lucky to get the job,' Philippa said lightly. 'If Simon and I aren't to stay here then. . . .'

'You'll live up at the Hall with me. That's what I've come here for, to take you both up there, and of course to make sure you haven't run out on me.'

'Mum, I've finished my breakfast. I'll go and finish packing.'

'Not very like Rivers, is he?' Scott asked derisively. 'He was blond, like you if I remember. Did you ever stop to think that we might have had a child?' he added on a savage whisper as Simon went upstairs, 'but then you didn't want my child did you? I couldn't give you all the things he could. But I *would* have given you marriage. . . .'

'Your grandfather would have disinherited you.'

'Do you think that would have mattered to me? I loved you, damn you,' he snarled. 'And anyway, it would have made no difference. I left shortly after you had gone, and he did disinherit me.' He saw her expression and laughed bitterly. 'I had to buy Garston back from the National Trust. They were only too glad to get rid of it, it isn't old enough to be of much historic value and it's costly to maintain.'

'Where did you go?' Why was she asking him this? Why was she tormenting herself in this way?

'To America. I had a godfather there. He loaned me the money to start the company. I planned to take you with me, but you didn't know that did you? I had it all planned. He'd loaned me enough money for mother's operation and she was going to go and live with a friend, you and I were going to make a new life for ourselves in the States, I knew there was no way my grandfather was going to let me have Garston, no way at all. Once I let him see how much I wanted it, he was determined to keep it from me. I used to think there was nothing of him in me, but I learned differently when you tricked me, I learned the hard way how the iron enters a man's soul, corroding him with bitterness. He punished me by withholding from me what he thought I most wanted; take care that I don't ever find out what you treasure most, Philippa.'

'God, you're hard. . . .'

'I'm what you made me,' he corrected cruelly, 'Do you feel proud of your handiwork? Does it give you a thrill to know that you and you alone are responsible for what I am today? When you left I had nothing. . . .

'I laughed when I heard Rivers had ditched you and married someone else. Can you believe that?'

'Very easily,' Philippa told him dryly. She was both fascinated and revolted by what he had become. Knives of fear and panic twisted in her stomach and she wanted to protest that he was wrong to feel so bitter; that she had acted purely out of love for him and nothing else. Where had it all gone so wrong? His grandfather had been so sure he would marry Mary, it hurt to think that she had given him up for nothing. Perhaps if she had been older she would have seen that he could never be a man to do another's bidding but she had been young and very, very frightened. She had thought of herself as some dreamy novelette heroine, sacrificing her own happiness for that of her lover, but all she had done was sacrifice both of them ... no, all three of them, she thought, remembering Simon's pale, unhappy face.

'I'll have to get in touch with Simon's school and arrange to sub-let our flat ... I've already spoken to my boss, but. ...'

'You can do all that from the house. I'll drive you down to the school this afternoon. Simon can come with us. Does he know whose son he is?' he asked stunning her. It was several seconds before she could get her breath.

'Yes,' she managed, telling the truth. 'He does know.'

'And he's forgiven you?' His lips twisted. 'It seems to me that Simon and I have something in common, you've cheated us both.'

More in common than he could possibly know, Philippa thought half-hysterically, glad when Simon came back downstairs, his eyes brightening when they fell on the car parked outside.

'Can I go and have a look at it?' The question was for Scott and not her, Philippa realised bitterly, wondering how on earth Scott was blind enough to ignore the almost startling resemblance between them when they were together, and wondering how long it would be before less prejudiced eyes did see it.

'You can look, but don't touch. ... I don't want that wrecking as well,' Scott cautioned dryly, watching Simon's thin face flush.

'If you're ready, we'll go,' he told Philippa, 'I'll send someone down to collect your stuff later.'

She had no option but to follow him outside, Simon bounding ahead of them, admiring the sleek lines of the car from every angle and then bombarding Scott with questions about its performance once they were installed inside. For once Philippa was glad of her son's excited chatter. It kept Scott's attention away from herself, and only she knew of the inner tightening of her nerves as Garston Hall approached, its chimneys visible over its protective circle of trees and then the front façade itself.

It hadn't changed, the same grey weathered stone still standing foursquare, the diamond leaded windows staring out towards the hills. Two wings protruded from the main block of the house, and Philippa remembered that these had been closed off when she had visited the Hall before. Now the windows sparkled and curtains flapped gently in the breeze. She half turned to Scott, about to voice her surprise, but he forestalled her saying coolly, 'One of the benefits of owning your own company—and a profitable one at that. I've been able to re-open both wings. One of them now houses the head office of the company, the other is used for any business associates I might have visiting me, and there's also a leisure complex there for the use of both staff and guests. The main block I have retained for my own use.'

'You live there alone?' What on earth had prompted her to blurt that out?

'Why? Thinking you might take up where you left off?' His eyes slid to Simon, who was listening to their conversation although his face was averted. 'Not completely. My mother lives with me and her companion, as to the rest . . .' his mouth curved in a humourless smile, 'sometimes I live alone and sometimes I don't, does that answer your question?'

CHAPTER THREE

'THIS way.' Scott preceded them across the flagged area at the front of the hall, indicating a door in the East wing which was new to Philippa. Simon lagged behind, scowling darkly, and Philippa suppressed a rush of sympathy. Poor Simon; what had he expected, that Scott would immediately recognise him as his son? It was unfortunate that Simon should have seen his birth certificate, and the blame lay with her for naming Scott as his father in the first place, but she had been so distressed after Simon's birth, so lonely, so aching for Scott's presence, that she had given his name quite automatically, still drowsy from Simon's birth, barely aware of what she was doing.

Once they were inside the building and Scott was describing the work his company was engaged on Simon's attitude changed. As far as Philippa was concerned it was all way above her head, although she couldn't help admiring the way what she remembered as vast, empty rooms had been transferred into a luxury office suite. A smiling receptionist acknowledged their arrival and from there Scott had shown them round the other offices, Simon drinking in every word he said, asking questions which brought a quick frown of surprise to Scott's forehead and a curt, 'He's extremely bright,' in an aside to her when he saw that Simon's attention was elsewhere.

'What did you expect? That because he was my child he would be dim?' How angry he was making her with his hateful assumptions. Couldn't he see what was screamingly obvious to her? Couldn't he recognise himself in Simon?

'This is where most of the real work is done.' It was a large room running the length and breadth of the wing, on the second floor, full of banks of computers and other pieces of equipment all totally incomprehensible to Philippa, but Simon was pouncing on them with glee, studying them with a keen-eyed fascination that drew smiles from the two young men working busily among the equipment.

'This is where we test out the new equipment. It isn't manufactured here of course. That's done in our factory near York, but we perform most of the field tests on the equipment here.' Simon interrupted with several questions which Scott answered, both of them involved in a discussion far too technical for Philippa to begin to follow. 'You're interested in this sort of thing I take it?'

'He's interested in anything he can take apart and put back together again,' Philippa said wryly, remembering the first time she had come home and found their ancient television set in bits.

'Umm, not something he's inherited from Rivers,' Scott remarked acerbically to her whilst Simon's back was turned. 'As I recall he was quite happy to play the playboy on what daddy had earned.' Before she could make a retort, he added, 'We'll leave Simon here and I'll show you my own suite, it's on the next floor.'

She had expected something even more luxurious

than the suite of offices on the ground floor but to
her astonishment Scott's office was almost monas-
tic in appearance. Another office led into it, and
this would be hers, he told her, gesturing to the
banked telephones and the word processor on the
desk. 'My previous secretary couldn't stand the
isolation of working here, and I need someone
experienced enough for me to rely on. I have to go
abroad quite frequently, and it will be up to you to
take care of things when I'm gone.'

'You trust me to be able to?'

There was a wealth of fine irony in her voice,
but Scott didn't take her up on it, merely saying,
'You come very highly recommended. You've
worked for Sir Nigel, who's reputed to be one of
the hardest-headed businessmen around. I don't
think he pays you simply to sit around looking
pretty.'

'How long do you intend to keep me here?'
Philippa demanded, reminding him that she wasn't
here of her own free will. 'Until you can find
another secretary?'

'As long as it takes,' he told her unequivocally,
'and remember, Philippa, whilst you're here you'll
fulfil any role I give you, that was part of the deal.'

What exactly did he have in mind? Philippa
wondered as he showed her the Directors' dining
room and the conference room which lay beyond
his own. Last night when he had given her his
ultimatum she had seen in his eyes a look which
had stripped her body of every shred of clothing
she had worn, and which had committed even
worse outrages against her, but she had put his
violence down to his shock at seeing her,

dismissing it in the calm light of morning as no more than a trick of her fevered imagination. Now she wasn't so sure. Scott ached to humiliate her as he thought she had once humiliated him and she would be a fool if she tried to deny that fact.

'I'll show you the other wing. It's this way.'

A long gallery connected the two wings, and the doors which Philippa remembered as once opening on to the main body of the Hall and the family's living quarters had been sealed off, apparently, because the wall was now blank, presumably to ensure that Scott had privacy when he retired to his own part of the house.

'Did you plan to do this when you . . . when you left for America?' she asked him, feeling slightly foolish when he turned and subjected her to an ice-cold, acerbic glare.

'I wasn't in any mood to plan anything,' he flung at her bitterly. 'I was aching too much from what you had done to me, Philippa. No, it was only when my grandfather died that I realised I might have a chance of getting the Hall back. I was doing quite well then, but it wasn't until two years ago that the company was doing well enough for me to buy it.'

They had reached the door at the end of the gallery and he pushed it open, standing back so that she could precede him. The doorway was narrow and Philippa felt the hairs on her arms stand on end as she brushed past his suit-clad body, the violent response of her nerve endings to his proximity so totally unexpected that it threw her off balance, both physically and mentally, and she was glad that she had her back to Scott for the few seconds it took her to get herself back under control.

What was the matter with her, for heaven's sake? She wasn't seventeen any longer. She had met many handsome and sexy men since she left Garston but none of them had affected her in the way that Scott had just done. Neither had he eleven years ago, but then she had trusted and loved him with innocence and inexperience, now she was immediately wary of the undeniably physical response of her body to his, her sense relaying to her the total maleness of him, the faintly arousing scent of his body whenever he came close to her, the diabolical ease with which her mind supplied her with an image of his unclothed body, even to the extent of adding the changes that time would have brought, turning him from a boy to a man.

She had to stop thinking like this. What was the matter with her? Had she gone crazy? How he would gloat if he knew what she was thinking. It was computers he made, not spells, she reminded herself wryly, and if she was acutely aware of him the responsibility for that was hers, and not his. He had done nothing to excite that awareness, and if she was wise she would do nothing to increase it.

She kept silent as he showed her over the West wing, now converted into five guest rooms each with their own private bathroom, a communal dining room, plus another room furnished for relaxation with large settees and a television. On the ground floor was the sports complex Scott had mentioned; an indoor squash court, a room with a snooker table, a conservatory complete with a huge swimming pool, and beyond it the outdoor tennis courts.

'It isn't easy getting the right kind of staff to work somewhere as isolated as this, so we have to provide a few inducements and of course they always come in handy when we're entertaining potential customers. I've got some due any day now as it happens, Americans to whom I'm hoping to sell the new computer we're working on.'

'Where will Simon and I be staying?' Philippa asked him as he walked towards the entrance. Sunlight splashed in through it, blinding her for a moment and she would have stumbled if Scott hadn't reached out to steady her. His fingers burned the bare flesh of her arm beneath the cuff of her short-sleeved t-shirt and she snatched it away from him, flushing furiously as his mouth compressed. 'You're both staying in the house with me. This way.'

The entrance hall was much as she remembered it, although now the parquet floor was properly polished as was the round table adorned with an attractive display of flowers. The doors to the right and left of the hall led to the drawing room and library respectively as Philippa already knew. To the rear of the hall a pair of matching doors led to the dining room and a small sitting room with the kitchen to the rear. 'I did away with all those small rooms and had the kitchen modernised. It made it much easier to get staff for one thing.'

'You say your mother is living with you?'

'Yes. I needed someone to take charge of the domestic side of things for me, although mother says I ought to get married. She complains that it's too much for her, even though she has Claire, her companion, to help her.'

'She had her operation then?'

'Yes.' His voice was terse as he added, 'Much you would care. Was that why you ran to Rivers, Philippa? Did the thought of being burdened with an invalid mother-in-law as well as an out-of-work husband frighten you too much?'

'It's over, Scott.' Philippa tried to sound calm and in control. 'I wish you could accept that, for your own sake.'

'For *your* sake, don't you mean? How does it feel, knowing that you're completely within my power, and knowing how you destroyed me? Doesn't it frighten you, Philippa, thinking what I might do?'

'I can't help it if you have a chip on your shoulder, Scott.'

'I can't help it,' he mimicked savagely, grasping her shoulders and swinging her round to face him. His eyes were dark and burning, just as she remembered them from the day she told him that she couldn't marry him and why. 'Don't give me that, you two-faced little bitch. Whose fault do you think it is that I'm carrying this "chip" as you call it? Well?' He was shaking her almost violently, letting her go so suddenly that Philippa staggered back against the panelling, jolting her shoulder so painfully that she had to suppress a cry of pain.

'Hurt, did it?' Scott asked succinctly, 'Don't try deceiving yourself, Philippa, I'm not the soft-hearted fool you tricked so easily with your soft voice and hands, I'll enjoy inflicting pain on you. I ache to see you hurting . . . ache. . . .'

'This will be your room.' They were upstairs, and Philippa quelled a feeling of stepping back in time as Scott flung open a door. Nothing had changed, the room was exactly as she remembered it, his room. Her eyes were glued to the bed. Scott's bed, an ancient fourposter. She shivered, as memories swept back over her. Scott kissing her, Scott undressing her, Scott making love to her, worshipping her shy body with his tender mouth and hands, just as she had worshipped his.

'But this is your room.' She hadn't realised she had said the words until she saw the bitter contempt in Scott's eyes.

'So you remember it then? I thought you would have been in so many since you might not recognise it. It *was* my room, Philippa; after what you did to me I couldn't bear to sleep here any longer. It made me sick to remember taking you here, feeling your body's response to me whilst all the time it was all a meaningless lie from a little slut who thought she was exchanging her virginity for a wealthy secured future, and who ran out on me the minute she discovered the truth. My grandfather told me, you see,' he said quietly, unleashing the savagery of his anger as she turned towards him, mystified by what he was saying. 'He told me that he sent for you and told you he would disinherit me, and he told me how you demanded money from him, how you told him that you would find another lover, someone rich enough to support you in the style your greedy, amoral little heart craved. He laughed at me when I said

I didn't believe him. Here in this room he took my pride and broke it, after you'd confirmed to me what I'd told him were malicious lies. Can you wonder that I couldn't sleep in here any longer?

'But *you* will, Philippa, and when you do I'll be praying that you'll be visited by the ghosts of the people we once were, because if there was nothing else there was pleasure between us, and I bet I could take your beautiful, faithless body now and pleasure it until you were ready to promise me anything. You see it wasn't only computers I learned about in the States.'

She wasn't going to respond as he expected her to. She wouldn't cry, or lose her temper, she wasn't going to pander to the need to draw blood she could sense building up inside him, and he would never know what it cost her to walk over to the window and say calmly, 'If this is my room, where is Simon's?'

'On the next floor.' He saw her glancing at the secondary door set into the wall and smiled mirthlessly. 'Ah yes, that door leads to my room. You see I didn't move very far away.' He saw her eyes go to the lock and laughed softly, 'And yes, I do have the key. Like I said, whilst you're here you'll perform whatever duties I might require of you.'

'I won't sleep with you, Scott.' She said it positively, not giving in to the terror she could feel stalking her, invading the room, cloaking her in ice-chilled fear.

'You won't be asked to,' he assured her as he turned towards the door. 'I'm going to my office.

You can have the rest of the day off to get settled in. Dinner is at eight, you needn't bother to dress.'

'Is it all right if I use the phone?'

'Why?' Something flickered in the back of his eyes, something hot and dangerous. 'Who do you want to ring? One of your lovers?'

'Simon's school.' She was struggling to hold on to her self-control to beat off the miasma of apprehension she could feel enshrouding her.

'Very well. I've already spoken to Dr Philipps and he's agreed to take Simon on as a pupil. No doubt it won't be long before his fellow pupils know of his illustrious paternity. You can't hide a thing like that in a village this size.'

Something in his bitterness destroyed her hard-won self-control. Without being aware of it Philippa took a step towards him, her body tense, her fingers curled tightly into her palms. 'If you do anything to hurt my son, I swear I will kill you, even if I have to do it with my bare hands. You can try to punish me as much as you like, but if you hurt Simon. . . .'

'What's the matter? You've said he knows who his father is?'

'Yes.'

'Well then what are you worrying about? If he knows Rivers' identity, presumably he knows he's illegitimate and that Rivers has married and has two other children beside him. Not that he spends much time with them. The boy's at prep school and the girl has a nanny. And Philippa.' She was still standing close to him and she recoiled as his fingers slid down her arms, circling her wrists, biting into her slender bones. 'If you ever dare to threaten me again,' he said silkily, his breath brushing the soft tendrils of hair at her nape, 'you'd better be prepared for the consequences. . . .'

She was just about to demand 'what consequences' when she realised what he intended to do. Panic coiled and exploded inside her as he pinned her arms behind her back with one hand, the other sliding up into her hair and tightening into it, pulling her head back, until the slightest movement tugged painfully on her scalp.

He took his time, lowering his head towards her slowly, mercilessly scrutinising her face for the signs of fear she refused to show. 'Well, well,' he breathed softly, only inches away, 'I did make a misjudgement, didn't I? Perhaps this is what you really liked all along . . . sex spiced with violence, is that it Philippa? Then you should like this.'

She was given no opportunity to resist, his mouth, hard and unyielding forcing her lips to part, bringing the rusty taste of blood to her mouth as she tried to withstand him and was punished by the grinding pressure of his mouth forcing the tender inner skin of hers back against her teeth. She made a muffled protest, lost against his mouth, hating him with a bitterness that threatened to sweep everything else away, forcing herself to cling to the memories of what he had been, instead of admitting the frightening reality of what he now was. It was a kiss that was a desecration of all that they had shared; of her tender and shy submission to him; of Simon's conception which had been a sharing and meeting of their souls as well as their flesh; and yet in spite of everything something inside her twisted and took fire, a spark which burned briefly before it was extinguished so that when he eventually lifted his mouth, and she became aware of the rough sledgehammer blows of his heart against her body, she was filled with self-disgust, with aching shame that she should have actually experienced in such a violent and destructive embrace, a fierce tug of sensuality that she had never known in the caresses they had exchanged before.

'Just remember why you're here, Philippa,' he warned her as he left. 'Don't try my patience too far. Not unless I'm right and you do enjoy being abused.'

When he had gone she refused to cry. She refused to do anything which would allow her to give way to the emotions he had aroused. Instead, she picked up the phone. Half-an-hour later, feeling decidedly calmer, she decided to go and look for Simon. She had arranged for their clothes and personal belongings to be sent on by her next-door neighbour. The flat would be sublet, Simon's headmaster had expressed his approval of her plans, and now all she had to do was to convince herself that she had never, not even for a second, felt anything in Scott's arms other than revulsion and horror.

Her memory of Scott's degrading embrace faded when she discovered that Simon seemed to be missing. One of the men in the computer room told her that he had gone to look for Scott. 'Ask Hank Brierly, Scott's second-in-command, he might know where he is. His office is just down the corridor.'

. Hank Brierly proved to be a pleasant American in his late thirties. When she introduced herself as Scott's new secretary he grinned appreciatively. 'Well, well, things are looking up.' His smile faded a little when she asked about Simon. 'Your kid, you say. No, I haven't seen him. He could be with Scott, although generally Scott doesn't have all that much time for kids. Something or someone kinda soured him for the marriage and family bit a long time ago and I guess he's still suffering from the blight.'

When Philippa approached Scott's office she heard voices on the other side of the door, but in her anxiety about Simon she didn't stop to ponder on the wisdom of her actions, simply knocking briefly on the door and going in. A tall slim girl with long dark hair and a pert triangular face was standing beside Scott's desk whilst Scott himself perched on the end of it. Although she could not be sure Philippa could have sworn that before she came in Scott had been caressing the girl's hands. She was young, much younger than Philippa, perhaps only eighteen or nineteen, and a white hot tide of emotion swept through her, almost too fast for her to identify it. Jealousy? Why on earth should she be jealous?

Both of them were watching her, the girl angrily, and Scott.... She was hard put to describe the look in Scott's eyes. It was a combination of watchful scrutiny and a certain amount of gloating satisfaction, but both emotions were masked by the cold hauteur he evinced as she approached the desk.

'I don't remember giving you permission to

walk in here, Philippa. What do you want?' His insolent tone brought hot colour stingingly to her cheeks.

'I'm looking for Simon,' she said quietly, 'he seems to be missing, and I thought he might be with you. . . .'

'He wanted to look at the Ferrari and I told him he could—look that is, not touch.' She turned back towards the door, pausing only when he said, 'Oh, by the way, next time, before you come bursting into my office, just wait until you've been given permission will you. . . .'

It was the softly muted giggle of the girl with him that stung her pride raw as she closed the door behind her. She had been well and truly put in her place, and she was still seething inwardly from the effects of it.

'Gave you a rough time did he?' She realised that Hank Brierly was standing by her desk and smiled briefly, 'My own fault. He had someone with him. I did knock but apparently they didn't hear me and in future I'm told I have to wait for the "Open Sesame".' She made it sound flip but that was something she was far from feeling.

'Umm. Someone with him, that will be Cara Laine, she's the daughter of Buck Laine. Scott's hoping he's going to buy this new computer we've been working on. Scott's sunk a good deal of capital in it and where Buck Laine leads others always follow, so if he gets this order there should be others, but Buck isn't totally convinced. I suspect that Scott is trying to perform a public relations job on Cara.'

'She's very pretty—and very young.'

'She's also very spoilt and far from being the innocent her lack of years might lead you to believe,' Hank told her dryly. 'She wants Scott, and unless I'm mistaken he's going to find that selling computers to her daddy means selling himself to little Cara, but I could be wrong. It has been known to happen. Not often . . . but. . . .'

'You think Scott would do that. . . .'

'What? Go to bed with pretty deadly Cara to secure the contract? I don't know. He's ruthless enough, but I think he's also clever enough to know that once Cara gets her hooks into him she isn't going to want to let go. She wants to marry and she seems to think Scott is ideal husband material.' His voice held a note of pain that puzzled her.

'He told me that his mother said he needed a wife.'

'Umm . . . but I doubt that Cara is what she had in mind. She was probably thinking of someone who could crack that tough outer shell, and turn him into a human being again.' He raised his eyebrows and grimaced faintly, 'I think I should get back to my office. Somehow I don't think our lord and master would approve if he came out here and caught us talking about him.'

It was said in a friendly fashion, but Philippa's nerves, still raw from her last two encounters with Scott, flushed. 'No, you're right, of course, and I must go and find Simon.'

'How old is he?'

When she told him he looked flatteringly surprised, 'Ten, you don't look old enough.'

'I was,' she assured him wryly. Old enough to

make love, but not old enough to know how to protect herself from the consequences. Sighing she went to find her son, thinking it was ironic that it was those very qualities and interests he had inherited from his father which had, in a roundabout fashion, brought both of them here within Scott's powerful ambit. When would he let them go? When he had finished tormenting her? She remembered the scene she had interrupted in his office. What were his real feelings about Cara Laine? Was he attracted to her, or was he simply using her? Cara wanted to marry him Hank had said. A cold shudder ripped through her body. What did it matter to her who Scott married? It was no business of hers, no business at all!

She didn't go downstairs for dinner. She went to the kitchen instead and managed to persuade Mrs Robinson, the cook, to let her and Simon share high tea at the kitchen table. Afterwards she took Simon up to his room, where they both stayed watching television until she was sure it was safe to emerge from the sanctuary of Simon's room and go to her own.

Once inside she checked the lock on the communicating door. It was reassuringly closed, and Scott no doubt was downstairs entertaining his mother and his American guest. Was she staying in one of the guest rooms in the West wing or was she more intimately quartered in the main building, perhaps next door to Scott?

Her room had its own adjoining bathroom, and she was tired enough after she had bathed to want to go straight to bed, without reading as she normally did. The day had been hot with thunder growling faintly in the distance; too hot for her to want the clammy stickyness of her nylon nightshirt next to her overheated skin. Eyeing it distastefully, Philippa dropped it on the chair beside her bed, sliding instead between cool cotton sheets, and stretching sensually, enjoying the cool brush of the fresh fabric against her tense skin. She wasn't going to remember how she and Scott had made love in this room, in this bed, filling the silence with their whispers and promises. She closed her eyes, willing herself to fall asleep mechanically counting sheep and wondering why it was that there was always one which refused to jump the gate. By the time she had backtracked to include it in her counting she was on the verge of sleep, submitting gratefully to its lure.

She wasn't sure what woke her; something which left her heart pounding and her mouth dry, her first thought that it must be Simon stilled, as she realised he was too far away from her to have heard him even if he had cried out for her.

'So you *are* awake.' The disembodied voice reached her from the corner of the room, jerking her body into total wakefulness, the sheet falling away as she sat up automatically, turning towards the communicating door which now stood open.

'Scott?'

'Who else?' he taunted. 'Who did you expect? Hank?' He rooms in the village!

'Scott what are you doing in my room? His intrusion had ceased to be funny and she stared impotently at him as he came towards her. The moonlight through her thin curtains revealed the contours of his body, gilded in silver, potently masculine, with very little concealed by the terry robe he was wearing. His hair was damp and she could smell fresh soap and clean skin.

'Scott, what do you think you are doing?' she repeated nervously. He was reaching casually for her bedclothes, flicking them back, pausing, his hands on the belt of his robe.

'I should have thought it was patently obvious, I'm getting into bed with you. . . .'

'But you said you wouldn't. . . .'

'Sleep with you?' She saw the white flash of his teeth but guessed there was no real amusement in his smile, 'Neither will I, the sort of relationship we shall have precludes the pleasure of sleeping together, but I do have certain needs, and you. . . .'

'For God's sake Scott, you can't mean this,' Philippa broke in, horrified.

'Oh but I do, and you must have expected me,' he said smoothly, 'otherwise why would you sleep with nothing to cover your delectable body other than my sheets? You knew what you were accepting when I told you what I would demand. Tonight I need a woman.'

'Then go to Cara,' Philippa said furiously, 'I'm sure she'd be only too glad to . . . to accommodate you. . . .'

'Doubtless she would, if I was prepared to meet her price. Cara wants marriage, whereas you . . . you aren't in any position to demand anything in return for my enjoyment of your body, and I *will* enjoy it Philippa.'

'I'll scream!'

He shrugged off his robe and her breath was caught and smothered by the male beauty of his body. 'Go ahead, no one will hear you. My mother sleeps on the next floor with her companion, as does Simon. In fact I think I might enjoy it more if you did scream although we both know there can only be one outcome. Does it bring back memories for you, lying here in my bed, like the virgin sacrifice you once were?' He wrenched back the covers before she could stop him and it was his turn to study her body, although there was nothing covert about his inspection of her silver-white limbs.

'I don't want to remember,' Philippa breathed bitterly, 'You're desecrating those memories, Scott, you're destroying them. You. . . .'

'No, you can't destroy what was only an illusion,' he said roughly. 'Don't try and deceive me again, Philippa.' He was on the bed, and she realised that he meant to make love to her, and moreover that there was no way she could stop him.

'Is this how you mean to exact your revenge, by using my body. . .?'

'This is only the start of it; this is the private side of it; the tip of the iceberg, the rest will come later. You humiliated me publicly, Philippa, I want you to remember that, and besides, what makes you think you won't enjoy this?'

'How can I when you're doing it to hurt me?'

'Oh, very easily,' he said softly, 'You see I intend to make sure that you do. I want you melting in my arms, Philippa, pleading and begging me to take you, and I warn you now I'm not going to be satisfied with anything less.'

CHAPTER FOUR

'SCOTT, don't do this.'

'That isn't what you said to me eleven years ago.' His face loomed darkly over hers as he pushed her down on the bed, the same cold fury burning in his eyes which she had witnessed earlier. Fear raced from nerve ending to nerve ending as Philippa fought against him.

'You aren't the man you were eleven years ago.' The words were whispered between her tortured efforts to breathe. 'This is rape, Scott.'

'No.' His lips were bared in a grin that reminded her of a wolf before it attacked its prey. 'This is what you owe me, Philippa. Night after night, week after week, month after month I dreamed about you, about how you had been in my arms. For eleven years you've haunted me, making it impossible for me to trust any member of your sex, or my own judgement where women are concerned. You and you alone are responsible for the fact that I don't trust the female race, and now you're going to pay.'

'How, by you raping me?' Somehow she had to make him see what he was doing. She had to reason with him and persuade him to let her go. The Scott she had loved could never have acted like this. Never, and all her instincts urged her to hold fast to her memories. Surely that Scott couldn't have disappeared completely, taken over by this cold, dangerous man who seemed to have taken his place?

'I've already told you, it won't be rape. We were lovers once, Philippa? Remember?'

'But we aren't the same people we were then.'

'What are you trying to tell me? That you're suffering from regret?' He laughed harshly, the sound thrown back at them echoing faintly round the large room. 'Oh, no, you won't escape that way. You owe me this. Did you ever think about me when you were with Rivers? Did you think about me whilst you were conceiving his child? Simon could have been our son.'

Was he really so blind that he couldn't see the truth? She remembered how she had longed for him to come after her, when she had told him it was over between them, and demand that she stayed. She had hoped against hope that he would refute the lies she had forced herself to tell him; that somehow he would know that she could never give herself to anyone but him, but she hadn't become bitter when he had believed her; she hadn't allowed his desertion of her to fester over the years. Instead she had held tight to the knowledge that he had loved her, and of course she had had Simon, whereas Scott had had nothing, but the pain of believing himself rejected by her.

Yes, she could see that it was possible that her behaviour could have sown the seeds of distrust of all women for him. He had loved her very intensely; just as she had loved him. It was useless crying over the past, as useless as crying for the moon but nevertheless she felt the tears welling in her eyes, and turned her head, but not quickly enough. The moonlight revealed the damp tracks to Scott's keen gaze and he laughed softly, the sound chilling her body.

'Tears? You cried before, the first time I made love to you, do you remember?'

A shudder she couldn't control ripped through her body and Scott laughed again. 'Ah yes, of course, a woman always remembers her first lover, even a woman like you. Do you remember what I did then, I wonder?' He bent his head in a parody of the comfort he had given her over eleven years ago, his mouth brushing her tear-damp cheek, his tongue roughly warm as it brushed away the salt moisture. One hand was cupping her face whilst the other held her down against the bed. 'You gave yourself to me with such sweet innocence, or so I thought, that I was wracked with guilt afterwards. When you cried I wanted to cry with you. The thought that I had caused you pain. I would have left you then but you wouldn't let me. You wound your arms round my neck and whispered to me that it could only hurt the once and that you wanted me to make love to you again. I suppose I ought to have guessed then.'

'Guessed what?' Phillipa tried to wrench herself away but he was too quick for her, pinning her to the bed with the full weight of his lower body, whilst his fingers pinned her wrists as she fought to escape from him. 'That because I loved and wanted you I was a raving nymphomaniac?'

'You said it, and as for love. . . .' He laughed harshly, 'I just happened to be in the right place at the right time, didn't I? Had I been a little older and more experienced myself I would have realised that it was cold old-fashioned curiosity that motivated you and nothing more. But I wasn't enough for you, was I? You didn't want a lover, you wanted to experiment, only it all came crashing down around you when Rivers ditched you, didn't it?'

'Scott, we could talk about this for a thousand years and it wouldn't alter anything. . . .'

'I agree.' He cut through what she had been about to say, his voice sardonic, his eyes watching her carefully. She had become accustomed to the darkness and could see the long lean lines of his body, his skin smooth and tanned. His robe had fallen open and her eyes followed the dark arrowing of hair; her body shuddering in unwanted remembrance of how she had once touched him, shyly, wonderingly, adoringly, blushing in confusion and pleasure when he shuddered beneath her touch, drawing her hands against his body, muttering her name between the spasms of pleasure he hadn't been able to control. Now he was very much in control—of everything apart from his burning need to hurt and punish her. He was like a man possessed—he *was* a man possessed! Philippa recognised suddenly. She closed her eyes in helpless pain only to be told, 'Look at me, Philippa, I want to see your eyes when I kiss you.' He bent his head and she made no move to avoid the punishing pressure of his mouth. He wanted her to fight him, but she wasn't going to. She was simply going to lie here and hope that he would come to his senses before it was too late.

But that proved easier said than done. When his

savage assault on her mouth provoked no reaction he changed his tactics. It might have been easy to lie stiff and unyielding beneath him when he tried to compel her response by force, but now with his mouth moving tormentingly against her own Philippa discovered that her fingers had balled into tiny fists, gripping the sheet beneath her as she stifled her instinctive need to respond. Make him angry an inner voice urged, make him angry and then you can fight him, and she started to struggle wildly against the constraining weight of his body. 'Lie still, Philippa,' Scott threatened, 'or do you want me to hurt you?'

She could feel the warmth of his breath fanning her skin and turned her head quickly to avoid any contact with him, tensing when she felt the light drift of his mouth against her face. Desperate to escape from him, Philippa arched her back to throw off the weight of his body, pummelling wildly against his chest with small fists, all the anger she had held at bay since he had brought Simon back to the cottage and thrown down his contemptuous ultimatum lending her a fierce strength.

Her rebellion caught him off guard, but it was only seconds before he managed to subdue the wild threshings of her body, using his superior strength to keep her pinned to the bed, lifting himself slightly away from her as his fingers fastened tightly round her wrists like steel manacles.

'You can't fight me and win,' he told her softly, 'but go ahead and try if you want to, but remember, I'm not giving any promises not to fight back.' He saw the brief flare of contemptuous anger in her eyes and laughed harshly, 'You're not that naive, Philippa,' he reminded her. 'You know damn well what you did to me, and if it's turned me into someone you don't like, well just try remembering that you're the one who's responsible. With very little encouragement I could take great pleasure in hurting you, both physically and mentally. When a man's betrayed by the woman he loves it affects him like that,' he added with soft savagery. 'I could very easily derive intense pleasure from watching you suffer.'

'By raping me, you mean?'

Dear God, how could they have come to this? What had happened to the gentle lover he had once been and the shy girl who had responded to him so tentatively? How had they devolved into what they were now, snapping savagely at one another; both longing to draw and taste blood, both filled with the same savage compulsion to wound? Scott's hatred of her must be contagious, because just for a second when she fought against his physical domination of her she had shared it, she had wanted to claw and tear at the smooth flesh of his body; to hurt him as he was threatening to hurt her, and in her anger all thoughts of fear and retribution had fled, but now they were back, and she wanted to plead with Scott to set her free, but her pride would not allow her to.

'The past is over, Scott,' she told him trying to keep calm. 'You must see . . . that nothing will be gained by acting like this. . . . Please be reasonable. . . .'

'Oh, I will be.' The soft assurance in his voice tensed her body in instinctive alarm. 'I'm going to do what any reasonable man would do in my position.' He glanced down at her, letting his gaze wander quite freely over her body, and Philippa realised what she had overlooked in her angry battle with him, namely that she was completely naked and the silver beam of the moon highlighted her skin erotically, emphasising her delicately feminine curves. She remembered that she had always been a little shy about letting Scott look at her before, and he had shown respect for her shyness, but there was nothing respectful in the boldly marauding way his gaze lingered on the pointed swell of her breasts. 'Remember how much you used to like it when I did this?'

He bent his head, circling her nipple lightly with his tongue. Almost instantly Philippa felt suffocated by the wave of sexual tension exploding inside her, her body rigid as she tried to reject her automatic response, her nipples peaking instantly into taut hardness.

It had been eleven years since Scott had touched her like that; eleven years during which no man had caressed her so intimately and yet her body's response betrayed how totally it remembered his touch. 'So, some things don't change.' Scott lifted his head, but in spite of the softness of his voice, there was no tenderness in his eyes. They were as cold and as hard as sapphires, staring intently into her wary ones, his thumb finding the erect hardness of her nipple and teasing it, whilst he watched mercilessly waiting for her response.

It came on the shudder that pulsed through her

body, taking her backwards in time, although surely she had never experienced this overwhelming physical compulsion that dominated her now. She had wanted and enjoyed Scott's lovemaking, but there had been none of this feverish hunger, this urgent need that wiped out everything else, reducing her to a quivering mass of nerve endings that reminded her so sharply that her body had its needs and that she had completely denied them for far too many years.

'If you don't stop this now, Scott, I shall hate you for ever.' It was a last desperate attempt to change his mind, and Philippa knew as he laughed, deep in his throat, a primeval sound of pleasure and triumph, that she had lost.

'Hate away,' he told her. 'It's a very powerful aphrodisiac, as I should know. What do you hate most, Philippa? This?'

His hand left her wrist and stroked slowly over her body, following the silver path of the moon. He shifted his weight slightly so that the rounded curve of her hip was revealed to him and the slender length of her thigh. 'Don't fight him. Don't do anything to encourage him,' an inner voice warned her, and yet her body screamed to her to be allowed to fight off the intruder who dared to treat it so familiarly.

'You loathe me doing this and that is why you tremble is that it?' His hand was still on her body, his fingers trailing lightly against her skin, her flesh no longer cool and still beneath their sure touch, but turning traitor, melting, burning. . . .

She bit down hard on her lip. What was happening to her? Her mind mocked the naiveté of her senses. Scott might have changed his feelings towards her but her body knew him as its lover, and nothing could change that. Nothing. A feeling of light-headedness swept over her, and it was several seconds before Philippa realised it was probably as a result of clenching her muscles so tightly, expending valuable energy which somehow she was unable to replace.

'Don't touch me.'

It was the last futile blaze of defiance she had left, and Scott seemed to recognise it as such as well because he turned his face from his idle scrutiny of her body to glance into her eyes as he said with a soft ferociousness, 'Before tonight is over you will be pleading with me to do far more than just touch you.'

'No.' Panic had entered her voice now, and as though it was the sign he had been waiting for Scott's mouth closed over her own, punishing it for the words of defiance that had slipped from it, tough fingers gripping her jaw, forcing her submission, the hard length of his body pressing hers down against the mattress, her puny attempts of her fists against his shoulders to force him to stop ignored as his mouth continued to plunder hers, numbing her body into weak stupor. When he eventually lifted his head she was trembling from head to foot, shivering beneath the careless caress of his fingers, stroking along the length of her body. She flinched as he moved but there was no violence in his kisses this time, just a blood-drugging, heat-inducing langour more dangerous than any amount of violence, offering a balm to her disordered senses, soothing them with a pleasure to which they responded before she could even think of stopping them. He kissed her trembling mouth, her closed eyelids, the soft, sensitive skin of her throat, biting the delicate skin lightly until she was shuddering against him, lost in the urgent tug of her own need.

The ability to think and reason left her abruptly and like an automaton she responded to the spell Scott was weaving so cleverly. He was right; she did still want him and her body overruled the urgings of her mind, remembering, not the years which separated them from their last coming together, but only that they had and that she had hungered for him ever since.

'You want me.' It was a statement not a question, and Scott slid his fingers into her hair, tilting her head back, pressing small teasing kisses at the corners of her mouth, tormenting its trembling outline with the moist touch of his tongue, watching her all the time so that he knew the moment the fierce blaze of need burned through her, and deliberately held off for a few moments longer, teasing her with the touch of his mouth, registering her small half moans of need and despair.

'Scott.' She said his name huskily, swallowing with an obvious effort, her eyes wild with all that she refused to say. Her hands found his shoulders, but they resisted the pressure she applied to bring him closer to complete the promise in the tormentingly light kisses he used to feed her hunger. A wild despair flooded through her and acting entirely on impulse she raised her head from the pillows running her tongue feverishly along the line of his collar bone, feeling the compressed muscle beneath her fingers, her breathing light and uneven at his lack of response. It drove her to a frenzy, her teeth biting sharply into the smoothness of his skin, her pulses leaping as she felt his faint shudder, her fingers trailing hotly over his body until they reached the barrier of his belted robe. She touched the fastening experimentally and then stopped.

'If you want to touch me, why don't you go ahead? You're not seventeen and shy any more, Philippa. You don't need me to show you how to arouse a man.'

Just for a second reality impinged, but as though he sensed what was happening, he ran his hand possessively over her body until it reached her breasts. Until he touched the smooth, swollen skin she hadn't realised how much she had longed for him to do just that. She breathed in deeply and sharply and made a small anguished sound in the back of her throat as his thumb brushed lightly over the pink aureole of her nipple. The room seemed to darken and whirl around her, a fevered heat coming off her body as she reached up, her fingers tense and uncertain as she found the fastening of his robe and slid her palm against the warm skin of his flat belly, her flesh sensitive to the rough scrape of his dark body hair as it touched her hand.

'Philippa.'

His hand found her breast and she moaned aloud at the fierce pang of pleasure that shot through her, giving herself up completely to the savage hunger of his mouth against hers, his tongue thrusting between her parted lips to savour the moist sweetness within.

As though his touch had unleashed something wild and elemental she moved sinuously beneath him, using her body instinctively to pleasure his, everything else forgotten as she gave in completely to the urgency of her need. Her reasoning powers completely suspended, there was only blind instinct to lead the way, to instruct her body in its reaction to the touch of his and Scott's harsh exclamation of pleasure as her hands touched the lean planes of his body, exploring and discovering the male shape of him only encouraged her fervent response. She didn't think about what had brought them together in this place, she didn't want to think about it, it was enough that they were here; that Scott was touching her with his hands and mouth, and that she was free to touch him in the same way, marvelling at the male texture of his skin; the male hunger she could sense within him, the unashamed response of him to her caresses.

She forgot that he had told her that he would make her plead for his possession and remembered only that this was Scott, her first lover; her only lover.

His mouth touched her breast, sparking off fierce pulsating pleasure, so intense that she cried out with it, locking her fingers in his hair, holding him to her. 'Scott, please. . . .'

'Please what?' His voice was slurred, his breath erratic and she was deeply aware of the pulsing heat of his skin.

'Please make love to me.' She wasn't even aware of what she was saying, or the triumph in his eyes, as he pulled her against him, bending over her, lean and dark, stroking her erect nipples with the rough lash of his tongue until she closed her eyes and cried out in feverish pleasure, reaching for him, wanting him to fill her aching emptiness.

When he did she was surprised by a brief, fleeting sensation of pain, sharp enough to make her tense. Scott checked, glancing down at her, but the pain was gone and she moved hungrily, arching her body up to meet him, kissing him feverishly, tasting the musky arousal of his skin, crying out with heated pleasure as he moved against her, and she picked up the familiar rhythm of his body.

Surely there had not been such exquisite pleasure before? Her body was still shuddering in the aftermath of it, still fiercely exulting in the heavy weight of Scott against her, his breathing harshly uneven, perspiration soaking both of them. He lifted his head and seemed about to say something, but Philippa could feel sleep claiming her, sucking her down into warm blackness. Scott was moving away and she murmured a small protest, curling up against him, clinging to his arm, not wanting him to leave.

The moment she woke up realisation hit her. She didn't have to open her eyes to be aware of the other occupant of her bed, her senses had already relayed the information to her.

'So you're awake.'

Scott it seemed had equally acute monitoring devices, and as though to confirm it he added, 'It's no good keeping your eyes closed and faking, Philippa.'

Dear God, how could she have allowed him to make love to her? Her mind cringed away from the pictures her memory was showing her with seemingly compassionless accuracy. She gave a small groan and squeezed her eyes tightly closed. What on earth had come over her? She started to sit up and then realised that she was naked, hastily tugging the sheet up to her chin, her eyes flying open as Scott said sardonically, 'It's a little too late for modesty now isn't it?'

'What are you doing here? I seem to remember you saying you didn't want to sleep with me.'

'In the end I decided I might as well.' Scott did not seem to share her desire to cover himself from her gaze. He sat up, stretching like a large lazy cat, the muscles moving sinuously beneath his skin. Philippa realised that she was holding her breath and expelled it hastily, wondering what time it was. It was daylight and she couldn't remember when she had last slept so deeply.

'So that you could gloat over me? Well you've had your petty revenge, Scott. It's over now, Simon and I are leaving this place.'

'Over?' His coolly controlled voice splintered through her hasty outburst, 'Oh no, my dear,' he drawled, leaning towards her, trapping her with the hands he placed either side of her head. 'Last night was just the first instalment, and don't try telling me that you didn't enjoy it.'

Her mind spun crazily, searching for an avenue of escape. That he should treat her like this was intolerable. She wouldn't allow him to play on her emotions and use her own body against her. Feverishly she hunted for some means of destroying his arrogant assumption that she was his simply for the taking, and then it came to her. 'Oh, but of course I enjoyed it,' she purred sweetly, watching his eyes widen and then narrow as he studied her. 'You see, I simply pretended that you were Geoff . . . just like I did before.'

'You did *what?*' He made an explosive sound in the back of his throat and swore under his breath, grasping her shoulders so hard that she cried out in pain. 'You. . . .'

He broke off as her bedroom door opened, his eyes turning to the door. Like someone trapped in a nightmare Philippa saw Simon walk into her room. He was dressed, his hair still tousled, and his eyes sleepy, but they sharpened instantly when he saw Scott in bed beside her, his thin face colouring up hotly, the door closing as he let go of it.

'Mum. . . .'

'Simon. . . .' She made a move towards him and then checked it, biting her lip as she remembered that she could hardly get out of bed. Scott made no attempt to move, simply watching them both and Philippa wanted to scream and rail at him that he could do what he liked to her but he must not hurt Simon.

'Simon. . . .'

'If you go downstairs and find Mrs Robinson, son, she'll fix you up with some breakfast,' Scott interrupted calmly. His words seemed to break through Simon's trance, the colour flowed back into his pale face and he stumbled back to the door. When it had closed behind him Philippa turned on Scott, her eyes burning with humiliation and pain.

'How could you do that to him?' she demanded. 'Couldn't you see how shocked he was . . .?'

'Why? Surely this isn't the first time he's seen you in bed with one of your lovers? He's ten years old after all, and you haven't been celibate for ten years, despite that very convincing little show you put on last night. You should save it for men who know you less well than I do. A mother of a ten-year-old son is hardly likely to be a virgin.' Philippa cringed beneath the lash of his contempt. Perhaps he felt justified in saying what he had, but it had been no play-acting. He had hurt her, if only momentarily. Simon's birth had been a difficult one and her body had taken several months to recover. 'Besides, seeing you in bed with me is something he's going to have to get used to whilst you're both living here.'

'You *want* to humiliate me, don't you?' Sour bile rose in her throat. What on earth had happened to her last night? She had known how much he wanted to hurt her, but she had let him storm through her defences; she had shown him how easily he could arouse her; how much she still . . . still loved him? Surely not?

'As you once humiliated me,' Scott reminded her. He raised his arm and glanced at his watch. 'It's eight o'clock, if you intend to be in the office for nine you'd better get up.' When Philippa glanced pointedly at him he leaned back against the pillows, his hands behind his head. The sheet had slipped down to reveal the tawny warmth of his skin, faint marks marring its smoothness on his shoulder where in her passion she had bitten him. Her own body was no doubt similarly bruised, and a wave of heat swept over her as memories of the night surged into her mind. 'I can't get dressed until you leave.'

'You mean you don't want to. You forget, Philippa, that I'm the boss, and I have no need to be at my desk at nine. It's up to you entirely, I'm quite happy to stay here all day, but I don't imagine you want Simon to come looking for you a second time. He's very easily shocked for a boy of his age and—er—experience, isn't he?'

His mockery of her son was the last straw. Philippa slid from the bed, too angry to care about her nudity, or the way Scott watched her as she walked over to the wardrobe. Her body was still sleek and supple, her breasts fuller than they had been when she was seventeen, her body more voluptuous, her skin pale and satiny, unconscious allure in the way she moved.

Something in the quality of the silence stilled her. She glanced round and saw that Scott was watching her intently. A silent message passed between their bodies, hers responding to it immediately, Scott's eyes smouldering hotly. He wanted her! She checked the heady feeling of power the knowledge gave her and gathered up her clean clothes.

'So it was Rivers who filled your mind last night was it?' Scott said softly, 'But I was the one who possessed your body, Philippa.'

'So you did.' She wasn't seventeen now and he wasn't going to quell her by reminding her of how vulnerable she was to him physically. 'But it's generally accepted among experts that the most powerful human sexual stimulant comes from the mind.'

'Meaning?' He said it softly, but there was no mistaking his banked-down rage.

Philippa glanced at the bathroom door and edged towards it, flinging over her shoulder, 'Meaning that I allowed my imagination to tell me that it wasn't you who touched me but Geoff. Now do you understand, or do I have to go on?'

She was in the bathroom, with the door locked securely behind her, before he could respond. She showered slowly, letting the water run over her skin, trying to blot out feelings and sensations from the night before. She still loved Scott. He had changed, almost beyond belief, but there was still something there, something which drew her with a compulsion she had never felt for anyone else. She had wanted him to make love to her, shaming though it was for her to admit it, and if Simon hadn't arrived when he did this morning he would have made love to her again. Despite her mental tension her body felt irritatingly relaxed; so lethargic and indolent that she felt like two separate people, her mind completely detached from her body, and fiercely resenting its voluptuous pleasure in Scott's lovemaking.

When she emerged from the bathroom he had gone and the communicating door was closed. Heaving a faint sigh of relief she went downstairs, wondering what on earth she could say to Simon. He was having his breakfast when she walked into the dining room, and greeted her rather off-handedly.

She had finished her grapefruit and was drinking her coffee when he fired the first salvo, blurting out, 'Why do we have to live here, why couldn't we have stayed in the cottage?'

'Because that's the way Mr Garston wanted it,' she replied formally, colouring hotly when she saw the arrogant disbelief in his eyes. 'Simon, our being here is not by my choice,' she assured him hotly. 'You know that. If you hadn't had that accident with his car. . . .' She bit her lip. It was no good blaming Simon for what had happened.

'Why was he in bed with you this morning?' Simon watched her steadily, 'Have you told him about me?'

'No. Oh, Simon. . . .' She pushed tired fingers through her hair, how on earth could she explain to him? 'I've got to work this morning, we'll talk about it later. . . .'

'Do you still love him?' He wasn't looking at her, his attention concentrated on the floor, and Philippa drew in a short sharp sigh. What on earth could she say? She had always tried to be truthful with him, and had always congratulated herself on their open relationship, but she was quickly discovering she had been living in a dream world. He had never told her for instance that he knew about his father. 'Yes . . . yes, I do,' she said shakily, 'but we can't talk about it now.'

'Is he still very angry with you?'

She seized on the excuse gratefully, 'Yes, Simon, he is and that's why he was in my room this morning. You see he feels that he must punish me because. . . .'

'Because you left him?'

'Yes,' Philippa agreed thankfully. 'Something like that. I'll have to take you up to the school soon, so that you can meet the headmaster. . . .'

'It's closed for half term,' Simon told her. 'Scott told me when I asked him.'

'Scott?' Her eyebrows rose, 'Wouldn't Mr Garston be more polite?'

'He *is* my father.' His face was sullen again and Philippa bit back a small exclamation. Everything was getting out of hand, running away from her. 'I've got to go to work now, Simon. I'll see you at lunch time. What will you do with yourself whilst I'm gone?'

'I'm going to watch them working on the new computer. Scott said I could,' he added defensively, 'and I want to. I like him,' he added stubbornly, 'even if he doesn't like you any more.'

CHAPTER FIVE

To her relief Philippa was too busy to spare any time on her own problems, and as the morning progressed she recognised that Scott hadn't lied about his need of a secretary. The previous girl seemed to have had little or no idea about filing, and Philippa found that she was kept busy simply sorting through the backlog of mail and familiarising herself with all the different systems.

Hank came in and showed her how to use the word processor, which thankfully she soon managed to pick up. He was congratulating her on this when Scott walked out of his own office and told Philippa curtly that if she had time to waste gossiping she could use it to make him a cup of coffee and take some dictation. He was no more difficult to work for than her previous boss, or at least he wouldn't have been were it not for her continual awareness of him as a man. While he seemed to be able to shut off the personal side of their relationship while they were working she could not. She was constantly aware of him, every sense heightened by his proximity. He had only to reach out towards her to take a file, or answer the phone and she was tensing in physical awareness, remembering what his body had felt like against her own, her mind full of disturbing visions of him.

At twelve o'clock her outer door opened and

Cara Laine walked in. The American girl was dressed expensively in a soft linen suit which Philippa thought privately was a little too old for her, like her hairstyle and glossy make-up. She gave Philippa a cold stare and said, 'No need to announce me, Scott is expecting me, we're lunching together.' She walked over to the inner door and opened it, calling out sweetly, 'It's only me, darling. I've come to collect you for lunch. . . . I spoke to daddy this morning,' Philippa heard her say as the door was closed. 'He's very keen to come and see you. . . .'

Was Cara's father as keen for a marriage between Scott and his daughter as Cara herself was, Philippa wondered, and then marvelled at the power of the mind over the body. She felt acutely sick at the thought, cold nausea seeping through her body. Scott marrying Cara, she couldn't endure it. She didn't look up when she heard the door open, although she was actually conscious of Scott as he walked past her desk, his fingers cupping Cara's elbow, his dark head angled attentively towards her. Did he enjoy taking her to bed, she wondered savagely, impaled on the spears of her own jealousy and hating herself for the intimacy of her thoughts. She had never felt like this about anyone, never; in the past Scott had not given her any cause for jealousy and she didn't like the discovery that she was capable of feeling it so intensely.

Damn Scott, and damn Cara Laine, Philippa thought impotently half an hour later, wrenching yet another piece of paper from her machine. Hank walked in just as she was putting it in her wastepaper bin and grinned humourously, 'Lack of blood sugar, that's what's the matter with you. How about joining me for lunch? The pub in the village do really good plain food.'

'Sorry I can't,' Philippa told him with a smile, 'I'm having lunch with Simon.'

'Umm. Nice kid, he was making himself useful in the computer room this morning. He's got a very receptive mind. Dave, our technician, was most impressed.'

'Yes, computers and motorbikes are the loves of his life at the moment. Scott's gone out,' she added awkwardly, 'with Cara . . . for lunch. . . .'

'She's probably heard the best way to a man's heart is through his stomach. I expect it's the first time she's come up against any resistance to her daddy's almighty dollar. Cara's been brought up with the idea that anything Cara wants, Cara gets. Her father is a widower and he dotes on her.'

'And you don't? Philippa guessed speculatively.

'She's eighteen for God's sake and acts like she's going on for thirty. If she doesn't quit playing around she's going to get hurt.'

'And that matters to you?' Philippa guessed. His thin features flushed. 'Yeah, it would.' He pushed his fingers wearily through his hair. 'Guess you must think me all kinds of a fool, it's plain she's got her sights set on Scott.'

'But Scott doesn't want to marry, or so you said?'

'No,' he agreed dryly, 'but he's a man like any other and knowing the way Cara's mind works, she probably thinks it's only a short step from his bedroom to the altar. Don't forget, Scott needs that contract from her father, and she isn't above using a little coercion.'

Her head was aching half an hour later when she left the office. She had worked hard all morning, but the moment she stopped her thoughts were immediately occupied by all her problems. She still had Simon to face, although he had seemed to accept the brief explanation she had given him this morning. She was gnawing on her bottom lip when she walked into the main block.

Mrs Robinson looked up and smiled when she walked into the kitchen. What did Scott's housekeeper think about her presence in the house? None of Scott's other employees lived in. Was she the subject of gossip and speculation in the village?

'Young Simon's outside with Mrs Garston,' Mrs Robinson told her. 'Round in the walled garden they are I think, Mrs Garston likes it there, it's sheltered and warm. It's her companion's day off today, but she and Simon seemed to be getting on like a house on fire. Still that's often the way of it, young and old finding a common meeting ground. If you wouldn't mind telling them that lunch is ready for me. It's fresh salmon, Mrs Garston's favourite.'

'Simon's too,' Philippa told her, adding wryly, 'not that he gets it very often.' Mrs Robinson didn't have the local accent, and obviously knew nothing about her and Simon, but Philippa wondered how long it would be before the gossip percolated through and how long before the housekeeper started to glance at her more warily.

She needed no directions to find the walled

garden, but nevertheless she listened carefully while Mrs Robinson explained how she could find it. As she crossed the cobbled courtyard at the back of the house and skirted what had once been the stables and were now garages, Philippa marvelled at the changes Scott had wrought. Where there had been neglect and untidiness all was now in order. From the stables a path led through the woods to the home farm. She had trodden it often enough on her way for milk and eggs from the farmer's wife, just as she had often met Scott in the sanctuary of the woods. In the autumn they were normally let out for the shooting rights, and she wondered if this was something Scott had continued. She could remember quite vividly how he had told her about his plans for the estate, for making it pay, but Computex seemed to have solved all his problems in that direction, and remembering his fierce love of Garston she wondered if he would indeed be prepared to marry Cara Laine to secure the future of Computex. Nothing changed she thought drearily as she walked towards the gate which opened into the walled garden. Eleven years ago she had wondered the same thing about Mary Tatlow. Then she had been wrong, but this time?

She spied her quarry long before they were aware of her presence. Eve Garston sat on an old wooden bench beneath the willow tree, Simon on the ground at her feet, listening raptly to something she was telling him. The smooth grass muted the sound of Philippa's approach, and she had reached them before either of them realised she was there, Simon's brief 'Hi mum,' mingling with Eve's pleased, 'Philippa, how nice, come and sit down beside me and tell me how you are. It's been so long. . . .'

'Eleven years. But I'm afraid I can't sit. Mrs Robinson has sent me to tell you both that lunch is ready. It's salmon, so both of you should be pleased,' she added unthinkingly and then flushed as guiltily as a small child, biting her lip when she saw the thoughtful look Eve Garston gave her. She had always liked Scott's mother and had felt acutely sympathetic towards her, guessing how she suffered under the domineering rule of her father-in-law. He hadn't approved of their marriage, or his second son's career, and she guessed that Eve had been made to suffer for her husband's defection, although she always seemed serene, despite the appalling pain of her arthritis. Had Eve known of her feeling for Scott? She had been too wrapped up in him at the time to pay much attention to his mother, it had been Scott's grandfather who had dominated all her anxious thoughts.

She was touched to see how easily Simon went to help Eve to her feet, matching his pace to her slow one. 'You have a very charming son, Philippa,' Eve told her with a smile, 'I've enjoyed our talk together.'

'Mum, Mrs Garston was telling me about her plastic hip joints,' Simon informed her, 'and all about her operation.'

'Not quite as dramatic as it sounds, but oh, the blessed relief from pain. Scott tells me that you're going to work for him as his secretary.'

'For a little while. Simon's headmaster thinks he

would do better in a small school environment and when Scott offered me the job. . . .'

Eve seemed to accept her explanation quite easily but Philippa noticed the way her eyes lingered on Simon while they ate their lunch, and the seemingly innocuous questions she asked Philippa about her life in London, although Philippa noticed she made no reference to her lack of a husband or Simon's lack of a father, so presumably Scott had told her about Geoff.

'You must be very proud of Scott,' Philippa said as they finished their coffee. 'He's done very well.'

'Mm . . . but I'd rather see him happy than rich. As a mother you will understand that.'

Philippa glanced at Simon's silky downbent head, his hair so like Scott's in texture and colour.

'Yes,' she agreed sombrely, 'yes I do.'

The afternoon passed swiftly enough with Scott returning at three to load her down with more dictation but she was glad to be kept busy and out of his sight, hating the elusive traces of Cara's strong perfume which clung to his jacket, tormenting with images of them kissing, perhaps even. . . .

Over dinner she met Eve's companion and instantly liked her. 'Simon and Philippa are staying at the house while Philippa is working for me,' Scott explained. 'It makes things easier all round.'

'It's nice to have a young face about the place,' Eve commented gently, 'I enjoyed our chat this morning, Simon, perhaps we can talk again tomorrow.'

'If you like,' Simon agreed, patently flattered. 'I could teach you to play draughts tonight, if you want,' he added. Philippa saw the twinkle in Eve's eye. 'I should like that very much,' she assured him. 'When shall we start?'

It set the pattern for the days that followed, and although on the surface all was calm and placid Philippa could feel the subtle tension crawling along her nerves. Scott had made no further attempts to enter her bedroom or to touch her in any way. If anything he was extremely remote. Sometimes in the evening he joined them for dinner, although more often he was out, usually with Cara Laine. Simon spent most of his spare time with Eve. He was back at school now and apparently doing well, although once or twice Philippa had caught him scowling darkly.

'What's wrong?' she asked him one night as she tucked him up in bed.

'It's that Cara Laine, they're saying at school that she's going to marry Dad.'

Philippa sighed, suppressing the words that sprang to her lips. Simon had taken to referring to Scott in this fashion, even though she had told him that he must not. 'Why not?' he demanded aggressively now, when she repeated her warning. 'He is my father, even if you don't want him to know it. It isn't fair, I have to pretend that I haven't got anyone but you, and I have.'

'Simon. . . .' If only she had never come back to Garston none of this would ever have happened. But was she being fair? Simon had known his father's name and would almost surely one day have wanted to find him. 'Simon, I know it doesn't seem very fair, but you have to think of Scott and Eve. . . .'

'You mean they wouldn't want me?' He was close to tears now and Philippa sighed.

'Oh, darling, I'm sure they would, but Scott wouldn't believe me, even if I told him. . . .'

'Is he still sleeping with you?'

Philippa caught back her shocked breath. 'Simon . . . No! I explained to you why. . . .'

'I don't want him to marry Cara, I don't like her, and besides. . . .'

'Besides what?' Philippa demanded gently, her heart aching for her son's pain. Of course he loved Scott, how could she ever have thought he might not, and of course he felt jealous at the thought of his father marrying someone else, having a family with her. She swallowed the huge lump in her throat, knowing that she shared Simon's jealousy. It had tormented her for days that whereas she should have felt pleased and relieved that Scott had made no further attempts to touch her, what, in reality she did feel, was pain and disappointment.

'Go to sleep,' she told him. 'It will all seem different in the morning.'

When she went back downstairs, intending to watch television for a while, she saw that Eve was already watching it. 'You look tired,' the older woman commented. 'Is Scott over-working you?'

'Not really; I worry about Simon.' She bit her lip, wishing she hadn't made that admission.

'Yes, it can be very difficult bringing up a child alone, especially a son. He's very like his father, unbearably so at times.' She looked up at Philippa who felt her pulses starting to thud, the blood thundering through her veins. She opened her mouth and closed it, grabbing hold of the back of her chair. 'He *is* Scott's son, isn't he?' Eve pressed gently, 'He's so very like Scott at that age, and of course it would explain so much. . . .'

Like why Scott had given her a job and had her living in his house? Dear God, what was she going to do?

'Scott doesn't know . . . about Simon, I mean. He thinks. . . . He thinks——' To her appalled dismay Philippa had started to cry, huge tearing sobs that hurt her chest, tears sliding impotently down her face.

'Oh, my poor Philippa!' How had she come to be in Eve's arms crying out her pain and anguish on Scott's mother's shoulder—the last person she should be turning to?

'I'm so sorry,' she gulped when the flood had ceased, 'I can't think what came over me.'

'I can,' Eve said dryly. 'My son can be the very devil at times, and I know for a fact that he's never forgiven you for what happened all those years ago. I must admit I was surprised—and worried when he told me you were going to work for him and live here. He's been so bitter. Of course he thinks I don't know about it. Sons always think their mothers are blind!' she grimaced faintly, 'and of course because of my health he always used to think he had to keep things from me, but I could tell. I guessed the moment I saw Simon that he was Scott's.'

'Scott thinks he's Geoff's son.'

'Does he indeed? And why I wonder, should he think that? Would you care to tell me?'

It was a relief to talk to someone about it. Eve

Garston listened in silence. 'Jeffrey always did hate Scott. He hated Scott's father, and he never forgave him for leaving home, for escaping him. When he discovered how much Scott loved Garston it was a weapon he couldn't resist using against him.' Eve sighed faintly. 'When Scott told me you were going to work here I wondered if he wasn't too much like his grandfather. He's been so bitter, Philippa.'

'Yes, I know but what could I do? I knew he loved Garston. . . .'

'And you loved him, so you decided that Garston was more important to him than you?'

'I was seventeen, romantic and full of day-dreams. It never occurred to me that his grandfather was lying to me, or that Scott wouldn't marry Mary. I thought I was being so self-sacrificing. . . .' She grimaced faintly.

'You played right into Jeffrey's hands, both you and Scott. My poor child, Jeffrey had no intentions of letting Scott have Garston, and when Scott told him flatly that he wasn't going to marry her he went a little mad, hurting him every way he could.'

'As Scott now wants to hurt me.' Philippa pressed her lips together and slanted a brief glance at Eve.

'Yes, I'm afraid you're quite right. I've been worried about that, more so since I realised that Simon was his. If he should find out. . . .'

'He wouldn't accept it.'

'No, possibly not. You know there's talk of him marrying Cara Laine?'

'Yes, Simon is very unhappy about it.' She saw

Eve's look and sighed. 'I wouldn't have told him, but he had seen his birth certificate—years ago, and when we came up here and he heard Scott's name,' she shrugged. 'I've explained the whole mess to him as best I can. He is very mature, but he's still a boy of ten, and I think he feels bitter and resentful because I've deprived him of his father. He worships Scott.'

'I've noticed.'

'Scott says he'll tell the police about Simon trespassing, and riding that motorbike, if I try to leave, and then there's the matter of the damage to his Rolls. I can't possibly afford to pay for it.'

'I'd gladly lend you the money, but somehow I don't think. . . .'

'It wouldn't make any difference,' Philippa agreed. 'I've come to the conclusion that the only thing to do is to let him take his revenge and hope that it purges the bitterness from him.'

'You still love him?'

'Does it show so very much?' she asked wryly. 'Yes. Yes, I'm afraid I do. Quite how much I didn't realise until I saw him again, but I have Simon to think of now. You won't tell Scott, about Simon, I mean?' she asked pleadingly.

For a moment Eve seemed disinclined to agree and she gave a faint sigh. 'I don't believe I have the right to. But Philippa, he is Simon's father, and if you could explain to him——'

'He would what? Accept me on sufferance!' She shook her head decisively. 'No. When the time comes I'd rather make a clean break.'

'And Simon—will he want to leave?'

She didn't tell Simon that Eve had guessed his paternity, but she couldn't help noticing how her son clung to Scott's side at every opportunity and how patiently Scott answered all his questions. He might not like *her*, but he was always scrupulously fair about not allowing his dislike of her to flow over to Simon.

'Scott's getting real attached to that kid of yours,' Hank commented one day. 'Funny how alike they are, both mentally and physically.'

Philippa shrugged, hoping he wouldn't notice her changing colour. 'Simon misses a father's influence, I suppose. Any news about the American contract?' she asked, changing the subject. It seemed to her that Cara was deliberately drawing out the negotiations, delaying things so that she would have more time to spend with Scott. If Scott was getting fond of Simon, Cara definitely wasn't. She complained waspishly to Philippa one afternoon that she was sick of him making a nuisance of himself.

'He's always hanging around Scott,' she told her. 'If the kid wants a surrogate father, why don't you go find him one? Who is his father anyway? Rumour has it in the village that it's some guy who ditched you to marry someone else.'

What else had rumour told her? Philippa wondered. Did she know about the relationship between herself and Scott? She suspected that she probably did; she certainly tried hard enough to make sure that Scott didn't spend too much time in his secretary's company. They were out together nearly every lunch time and she was constantly walking into the office.

One afternoon after work Philippa found Simon moodily kicking pebbles round the courtyard, hands stuffed in the pockets of his jeans, his face contorted in a scowl.

'How about a swim?' she suggested. They often used the indoor pool late in the afternoon, but Simon hunched his shoulders and shook his head.

'I was going out with Scott, he promised me, but *she* wanted to go out with him.'

'Simon, try to understand, Cara wants Scott to herself, just like you do. Adults do want to be alone at times you know. . . .'

'You mean she's in love with him, don't you? Is he going to marry her?'

'I just don't know, and it's really none of our business is it?' she added gently.

Simon rounded on her furiously, his cheeks poppy red, his eyes defiant. 'It is my business,' he shouted back, 'he's my father!'

She felt too dispirited to discuss it further. Eve and her companion had gone out to have dinner with friends, Scott was out with Cara, and so Simon and Philippa ate dinner alone. It was late when Scott got back. Philippa heard the sound of his car, and she had no idea when he came to bed; she was fast asleep, even though she had lain for what seemed like hours after the car had stopped, listening for the sound of his tread along the corridor. Had he spent the night with Cara?

She had been at Garston nearly a month now. They were having a hot spell, and she decided to have a swim after work. She was just on her way to her room to collect her swimsuit when she heard

Simon's voice, raised and bitterly angry, coming from the direction of the garage area. Frowning, she walked past the door and into the yard, coming to an abrupt halt. Scott and Simon were standing on one side of the Ferrari, Cara on the other. Both Simon and Cara were flushed and angry, and the American girl's voice was acid with scorn as she said tightly, 'Scott, for God's sake get rid of this damned kid. If you're so all-fired fond of them, have some of your own, I'm sure you're more than capable, darling, and you wouldn't have to look far for someone to share your bed. . . .'

'He doesn't.' That was Simon, struggling to hold back tears, unaware that Philippa was hurrying towards him. 'My mother already shares it,' Simon stuttered furiously, 'and they're going to get married, and . . '

'Simon!' Philippa was too shocked to do more than call his name, but he turned immediately, his face flooded with guilty colour and did something he hadn't done in years, running towards her and hurling himself into her arms.

'My God, so it's true,' Cara hissed venomously, 'I'd heard about it in the village, but I thought you'd seen sense, Scott, I thought you'd realised exactly what sort of woman she was. Well, I wish you well of her,' she spat out, 'but just remember when she's warming your bed in future, how much she cost you. There's no way you're going to get Daddy's contract now.'

She whirled into the house before Scott could speak, and Scott turned to Philippa, his face white, his eyes burning bitterly as they ripped savagely into her. 'Damn you,' he swore furiously. 'You always were trouble for me Philippa, you always were and you always will be!'

She was too concerned about Simon to take the time to point out to him that he could have denied Simon's shrill statement. The crying had stopped, but he was still shivering in her arms.

'You'll pay for this,' Scott told her angrily. 'You can damn well be sure of that.'

'What do you want me to do? Tell Simon to apologise to her? Was it my fault that he saw you in my room?'

'I never said a thing about marrying you. I suppose he got that from you, a sop to your conscience. Well, let me tell you. . . .

'No, let me tell *you*.' Philippa stormed back at him. 'Your precious Cara wanted to marry you and she was going to use her daddy's buying power to make sure she got you. Go to her now, I'm sure you'll soon be able to convince her it was all a tiresome mistake; just a silly jealous little boy who's become far too fond of a man who doesn't give a damn about the feelings of anyone but himself. Go ahead . . . what's stopping you?'

'That,' Scott told her flatly as they both caught at the same time the sound of the expensive engine of Cara's car firing up. 'Have you any idea how much you just cost me? I could lose everything, do you realise that?' He turned on his heel and left before she could say another word.

In the morning Simon was so wan and listless that Philippa told him to stay in bed.

'Don't worry about him, Philippa, I'll go up and sit with him for a while,' Eve assured her.

'You know what happened?'

'Not really. Scott came in in a foul temper before dinner and said that Cara had left and that we could say goodbye to the American contract. He said something about Simon causing a scene. . . .'

'Simon's been very jealous of Cara. She rubs him up the wrong way, deliberately I'm sure.' She couldn't admit even to Eve that for a moment she had half expected Simon to state that Scott was his father and that she was still having cold shudders at the thought of it. It wasn't fair of Scott to blame Simon and her for losing the contract though. He could easily have gone after Cara. Her storming out had been more for effect than anything else, and she had expected Scott to follow her, Philippa was quite sure. She had thought she had him over a barrel and perhaps Scott had sensed that too. And he was, after all, not the man to dance to any woman's fiddling.

CHAPTER SIX

'WELL, well, public enemy Number One,' Hank teased lightly. Philippa sighed as she removed the cover from her typewriter. 'Ah, you've heard about last night.'

'In vivid technicolour,' he affirmed. 'Cara came storming into the pub just as I was sitting down to eat. You've made yourself an enemy there.' He was watching her speculatively, and Philippa wondered how much credence he had placed on what Cara had told him.

'You must be pleased though,' she said dryly.

'You mean that with Scott out of the running she might turn to me? Could be. She's flying home in two days, and I've offered to go with her. She's convinced herself that she's a very fragile flower and right at the moment she needs someone to hold her hanky and dry her eyes. Scott owes me some leave and we're slack enough for me to be able to take it.' He frowned. 'Of course, it's going to create cash flow problems with this new machine. Scott hasn't got any more orders in the pipeline.' He glanced at his watch. 'I'd better go and clear my desk if I'm going to take time off. See you later.'

It was after lunch when the phone rang. Philippa hadn't seen Scott all day and she picked it up automatically. 'Pippa, my dear, how are you?' She gasped at hearing Sir Nigel's voice and wondered why her old employer was ringing. She exchanged pleasantries for several seconds and then he said convivially, 'I think I might be able to put a little business your new employer's way, my dear. Sheikh Raschid is over from Qu'har, and it seems he's very interested in equipping the police force with an up-to-date computer. It could be the first of several; they can certainly afford it. He asked me if I could recommend anyone, and I thought immediately of Garston. He does have a formidable reputation and he's working on something rather revolutionary at the moment isn't he? Is he there?'

'Not at the moment.'

'Umm, well Raschid is over here for a week, so that doesn't leave much time. Would you ask him to give me a ring when he comes back? I thought we might arrange a meeting, get Raschid up there so that they can talk to one another. He sends you his best by the way.' Philippa could tell that Sir Nigel was smiling and repressed a small grin herself. The charming liquid-eyed Arab had been very gallant to her on his last visit, and she rather enjoyed their very mild flirtation, even if she was too sensible to deceive herself that it was anything more than that.

'I'll tell Scott just as soon as he comes in,' she promised.

The rest of the staff had gone home before Philippa finally decided to call it a day. There was no sign of Scott's car and on a sudden impulse she headed for the woods, enjoying the playing of the light evening breeze across her skin, telling herself she was a coward for not returning to the house and facing Simon. For the sake of her son she must leave Garston, and she would have to tell Scott that. He had eyes, he could see how attached to him Simon was getting. He had already witnessed how dangerous it could be, surely he wouldn't refuse to release them now?

By the time the Hall was in sight again she was feeling much calmer, although she couldn't help wishing that neither Eve Garston nor Simon himself were aware that Scott was his father. Although she couldn't entirely discount the fact that Simon shared an interest in computer science with Scott, she wondered if he would have become so emotionally involved with him if he hadn't known that Scott was his father, and yet she couldn't find it in her heart to blame Simon. It was only natural that he should be drawn to Scott. No, if anyone was to blame it was her. Just for a moment she allowed herself to imagine how her life might have been if she had not listened to Jeffrey Garston; if she had not been seventeen and so innocently in love that he had been able to mould and use her as a weapon against his grandson. It was too late for regrets now, she reminded herself. Scott was too bitter for her to be able to approach him with the truth, and even if he wasn't her pride would prevent her from telling him. No doubt he would quickly accuse her of playing on his sympathies and she could hardly expect him to shoulder the responsibility of a child he didn't even know he had fathered. No, matters were best left as they were, although the sooner she and Simon left Garston the better!

Eve was dining out again, she had several

friends in the neighbourhood, and Philippa couldn't help comparing her gracious, kind manner with that of her boorish father-in-law. Jeffrey Garston had never been popular in the area, and Philippa suspected that there might be some truth in the rumour that his fatal heart attack had been brought on by his discovery that the grandson he had always hated had done so well for himself. Had he guessed that Scott would purchase the estate on his death? And Scott, did he ever regret doing so? She had seen how much it cost him to run the house; the rental from the home farm alone could never even have paid the rates. No wonder Scott was so anxious about this new computer, and she had, indirectly, been responsible for him losing the contract. There seemed no doubt that he had lost it, even Hank had believed that. His love for Cara didn't blind him to her faults; she could be vindictive as only spoiled teenagers could be and her father had never been known to refuse her anything she wanted.

When she returned to the house the first thing Philippa saw was Scott's car parked outside. That meant that he was back, and she wondered bleakly if he had perhaps been to see Cara, in an attempt to get her to change her mind. She suspected that the only thing that would change Cara's mind now was a wedding ring and Scott didn't seem prepared to offer that.

She went upstairs to find Simon still in bed, but looking much more cheerful than he had done that morning.

'You realise that you've been very, very rude, don't you, Simon,' she chastised him gently, 'and that it was quite wrong of you to say what you did?'

'It was true, he was in your bed, I saw him.' He sounded truculent and avoided her eyes. Suppressing a sigh Philippa took his hand. It was larger than her own, brown and thin, but still a child's hand.

'But it isn't true that we're going to get married, you know that Simon.'

'Well, I didn't want her to marry him. What will happen now?'

'Well, first you will have to go and apologise to Sc ... to Mr Garston. ... Cara is leaving tomorrow, so there won't be time for you to go and apologise to her.'

She saw the relief lighten the strain in his eyes and tried to squash her feeling of sympathy. It was very hard at times, being a single parent, there were some situations she just did not feel equipped to deal with and this was one of them. The trouble was that she shared Simon's feelings and yet she knew that she must make him see that his behaviour had been very wrong.

'Will Scott ... Mr Garston make us leave?'

If only he would, Philippa thought wryly. 'I don't know, Simon, we shall have to see, but we'll have to leave sometime you know.'

'I wish you would tell him about me.'

Here was the nub of the problem, and Philippa didn't know what to say to him. In other circumstances she could have approached Eve and asked for the benefit of her experience and wisdom, but Eve had her own axe to grind in this matter, and Philippa suspected would recommend that Scott was told the truth.

'Simon, I know how you feel, believe me, but I can't tell him. Not at the moment. . . .'

'Why? He's my father and I want to be with him. It's not my fault that you lied to him.' His face was flushed and Philippa could see that he was working himself into a distressed state. The dreadful thing was that she felt she had no defence. How could she explain to Simon the complexities of adult relationships or expect him to understand them? What if he decided to take matters into his own hands and to go to Scott himself? She shuddered, forced to face the fact that Scott would probably reject him. What damage would that do to Simon psychologically?

'Simon, I can't tell Scott about you while we're living here; that wouldn't be fair to him or to you. Please try to understand. You've known the name and identity of your father for some time. Scott has no idea that he has a son. It's bound to come as a shock to him, but I can appreciate that you feel he is your father and you want him to know, so, when we get back home, I'll write to him and explain. But only if you promise me that you won't say another word about this—to anyone—while we're here.'

It was moral blackmail, something she had always avoided, but what alternative did she have? To say that Scott would be shocked was putting it mildly, but how could she explain to Simon without increasing his distress that Scott was more likely to reject than accept him?

'All right then, but just a long as you promise to write to him?'

'I promise. Now would you like some supper?'

'I'm not hungry.'

Philippa had little doubt that he was punishing her, but she couldn't find it in her heart to blame him, and tiredness dropped on her like a heavy cloak as she stood in the door of his room and studied his thin hunched body, his head turned away from her. He was so like Scott, no wonder Eve had spotted it.

She had to walk past Scott's room to reach her own, and as she did so she caught the sound of activity inside, and remembered Sir Nigel's message. Her ex-boss had told her that he would be in his office until eight, which left plenty of time for Scott to ring him, but on impulse she knocked on Scott's door. He might be planning to have dinner out for all she knew and she didn't want to miss him.

She heard him call out a muffled 'Come in,' and turned the handle, opening the door.

The bedroom was empty, the door that led into the bathroom standing ajar.

'Yes, what is it, Mrs Robinson?' she heard Scott call from inside it, and tensed, her voice suddenly deserting her. A lean brown arm thrust the door open followed by the rest of him, the brief towel secured round his hips brilliantly white against his tanned flesh.

'Philippa!' Just for a moment he seemed shocked, and she had a brief, unguarded glimpse of the Scott she had once known, but almost immediately he recovered, his voice a taunting drawl as he murmured, 'Well, well, what a charming surprise. What happened. Did you get tired of your lonely bed? Or has young Simon been putting ideas into your head? Are you having second thoughts about my suitability as a husband? If you are I'm afraid you're eleven years too late. I'm a good deal wiser now than I was then.

Colour flared in her pale face, and she was acutely conscious of how tired she was, how hot and sticky she felt, her body burning beneath her t-shirt and skirt, her eyes drawn against her will to the damp expanse of Scott's chest. Dark hair formed a virile cross on his body and Philippa remembered with unwanted clarity the way her fingers had traced it not so very long ago. Her mouth was dry with tension and she touched her tongue nervously to her lips, shivering when Scott's gaze locked on the betraying movement, his eyes darkening until they were almost black.

'I've come to give you a message,' she told him hurriedly, 'from Sir Nigel, my ex-boss. He wants you to ring him. . . .'

'Why, to plead with me to send you back? Is he the reason your body trembles whenever I come near you, Philippa? Is he your current lover?'

'No!' The denial was wrenched from her and she stepped backwards nervously as Scott came towards her. She could smell the soap he used, every one of her senses alive to him as he stood over her. How could he be unaware of the effect he had on her? Shamingly her breasts responded immediately to his proximity, heat filling her veins, her body yielding meltingly.

'He thinks he may have a customer who could be interested in your new computer. . . . He wants to talk to you about that. . . .'

'Does he now! What's this supposed to be? Compensation for costing me the American contract?'

Angry colour flamed in her cheeks. 'Certainly not. If you must know, it's nothing to do with me, Sir Nigel's idea entirely. He simply thought he'd do a fellow businessman a favour. He isn't like you,' she added sarcastically, gasping when Scott's fingers grasped her arm and he hauled her round to face him. So close to she could see the fine droplets of moisture clinging to his skin, her nostrils full of the warm clean smell of him. She tried to take a pace backwards, wanting to put a safe distance between herself and the sensual torment of Scott's body, but his grasp on her wrist only tightened.

'No. I'll bet he isn't,' he grated, watching her closely. His face looked taut beneath his tan, his eyes darkening with a savagery that made her muscles tense and coil in mute alarm. 'But then he doesn't know the real you, does he, Philippa? He doesn't know how readily you sell yourself to the wealthiest bidder.'

'Just as you were prepared to do to secure the American contract,' Philippa flung back at him, too angry to heed the warning light glittering in his eyes. 'How sanctimoniously you criticise me, Scott, but you aren't exactly pure as the driven snow yourself, are you? Or are you going to tell me you are genuinely in love with Cara?'

'Love? That's an emotion you wouldn't begin to understand. Love is for fools and weaklings as far as you're concerned, isn't it? Tell me, have you ever actually loved anyone? Ever given anyone anything other than your delectable wanton body? Have you, Philippa?'

He was shaking her now, so caught up in his own anger that she sensed that he was barely aware of how much he was hurting her, his fingers biting deeply into her skin as he gave way to the rage simmering inside him and let it erupt fiercely, scorching her with words that burned like red hot brands.

'How dare you speak to me like that? Of course I've loved. I love Simon, I. . . .'

'You loved his father, is that it?' Scott demanded, thin-lipped. 'But he left you to bear his child alone, didn't he? He didn't love you enough to give you his name, isn't that the truth?'

'Yes. Yes, I loved Simon's father,' she agreed wildly, not allowing herself to think of what she was admitting. 'And if you want the truth, I still love him, I. . .'

She came to an abrupt halt just realising where her heated words were leading her, her eyes unknowingly hazed with pain. It was too late to recall her impulsive words and far, far too late to pretend to herself that she hadn't meant them. Scott's rage had set off an explosion inside her that had totally destroyed her defences, and now it was too late to recoil from the truth.

'You still want him,' Scott grated. 'Well, you're just going to have to make do with me, aren't you?'

His fingers imprisoned her wrists just as she lifted her hands to fend him off, forcing them behind her back and using this superior strength to propel her against the hard length of his body.

Fear skittered wildly inside her, her pulses thudding in sensual response.

'Scott, don't do this,' she protested, sensing the sexual urgency building up inside him, and wondering if it was anger that had sparked it off, or her tactless reference to Cara.

'Shut up, Philippa,' she heard him say thickly as he lowered his head, 'unless you want to make me even angrier than I already am. You owe me this.'

She jerked her head back, feeling the bones in her neck snap painfully, her manoeuvre to no avail as Scott anticipated her and used his free hand to grasp her, his fingers tightening into the thickness of her hair, holding her motionless and defenceless as his mouth bruised hers, his teeth nipping painfully on her lower lip.

She held out against him as long as she could, her body stiff with tension and anger, and as though he sensed that she would not give way beneath the pain he was inflicting on her, the pressure of his mouth eased slightly, the fingers clamped to her skull deftly massaging her taut flesh, soothing away the tension she was using to hold him at bay until she could feel it virtually flowing out of her body, to be replaced by a mindless, heady langour; a heat that warmed her skin and drained her resistance.

'I want you, Philippa, and you want me too, for all that you pretend you don't. . . .'

The words were muffled against her mouth but they hurt like tiny darts in her heart, inflicting pain, reminding her of what he really thought about her. She managed to pull away from him long enough to say bitterly, 'According to you I want most men I come into contact with. . . . How does it feel being one of a crowd?'

If she had meant to taunt him into releasing her with her bitter words, she had failed miserably Philippa recognised as the pressure on her aching wrists and the base of her spine increased until she was intimately aware of Scott's body, and its hardening arousal.

'Right now this is what I feel,' he told her thickly, watching the recognition dawn in her eyes and with it a sexual excitement she couldn't quite conceal. This was what love did to you, she thought weakly, it made you vulnerable, dangerously so. 'And you feel it too.' There was triumph in the mockingly spoken words and in the glittering eyes that searched her face for more evidence of betrayal. Scott released her wrists, his hand sliding up under her t-shirt, tracing the line of her vertebrae, making her body shudder deliciously in pleasure. She was dying, drowning in a vast, silent pool of warm water, drowning and not even wanting to do a thing about it. 'Philippa. . . .'

His voice was tense with hunger and excitement, his mouth hot where it burned against her skin; the tiny, thready pulse thudding in her throat; the exposed curve of her shoulder where his teeth nipped delicately at her soft flesh, his hand cupping the warmth of her breast, his thumb. . . . Reality shuddered through her and she pushed bitterly away, not knowing which of them she hated the most. He was destroying all that she held most sacred; all the precious tender memories she had held on to during the lonely years, savaging and destroying them with his experienced seduction of her senses, with his kisses that told her how much he wanted her and how little he loved her.

'Oh no, not this time. We're not playing that game again,' he warned her acidly. He took a step towards her and Philippa backed off instinctively, both of them shocked by the sudden intrusion of the brief rap on his door.

'I've brought up your tea, Mr Garston.' With Scott's attention deflected to the door and his housekeeper, Philippa was free to escape, using the communicating door between their rooms, locking it feverishly behind her, before subsiding on to her own bed, trying to ignore the dull ache that radiated from the pit of her stomach. She had wanted him and in another few moments she would have let him make love to her, regardless of how much he despised her.

She covered her face with her hands, trying to stop her body from trembling. Dear God, what had she come to? He was like a drug to which she had no resistance at all. He simply had to be in the same room and her senses reacted to him; when he touched her she went up in flames, and only the fact that he didn't know the truth about Simon and the past, could keep him from guessing exactly how much she still cared. And if he should guess? That was something so potentially humiliating that her skin crawled with heat and agony at the mere thought of it.

She was in her bathroom, showering, trying to suppress her potent memories of Scott's body clad in nothing other than that brief towel, when she remembered that she had never asked him to release her, or talked to him about her concern for Simon. It would have to wait for another occasion now and one, preferably, conducted in such circumstances that she would not be sidetracked from her purpose by the distracting ache of hunger that always seemed to enfold her when she was with him.

CHAPTER SEVEN

ON Saturday morning Philippa woke up early. She had promised to take Simon to York and needed to do some shopping herself. The very hot weather they were having showed up the deficiencies in her wardrobe, which was more geared to lower temperatures, and she was tired of wearing her one and only denim skirt for work every day. That wasn't the reason she was awake at half-past six though. No, the explanation for her inability to snatch more than a few hours rest lay on the other side of the communicating door, no doubt enjoying the dreamless and restorative sleep that was denied to her. Forget Scott if just for today, an inner voice urged her; forget him.

Unfortunately that was easier said than done, and as she showered Philippa found herself remembering how she had felt when he touched her; how her body had melted with a sudden onrush of heat that had stunned her. He wanted her he had told her and in his arms with his body enforcing its masculinity on her she had felt that wanting and known that it sprang from the same deep craving which motivated his desire to enforce his power over her. He enjoyed humiliating her, Philippa acknowledged wearily; and if he ever guessed how much she still loved him. . . . But if he knew the truth. . . .

If he knew the truth it would make no difference

that same inner voice warned her; all he would do was use it against her. He was too bitter . . . too hard for her to reach him now. He wouldn't surrender his resentment of her lightly; it had become an intrinsic part of him, something he needed to fuel his drive to succeed.

She shivered, half shocked by how easily she could dissect his deepest feelings. This was what love did to you; it gave you an insight, a power that was as much a pain as a pleasure. It brought her no pleasure to know that if she had not allowed him to think she had deserted him Scott would probably have never made his company the success if was. Bitterness, hatred, resentment had that effect on people; it made them hungry. Happy people, contented people, were people who laughed at ambition, who turned their backs on the competitive world. Happiness had never spawned an empire-builder.

She reached out for a towel, wrapping it round her body, tensing as she remembered the look in Scott's eyes that first time he had made love to her after he had forced her to come here. 'I pretended you were Geoff,' she had told him and there had been a look in his eyes then that warned her that her remark would not go unpunished. 'I want you,' he had said to her, and only she knew how close she had come to replying, 'I want you, I love you.'

Was that what he was doing, baiting the trap by using the desire he could obviously sense she felt for him, hoping to use it against her, forcing her to admit. . . . What? That she loved him? No doubt in his eyes such an admission would be fitting recompense for what he saw as her treachery all those years ago.

She heard her bedroom door rattle and stiffened, but it was only Simon, come to see if she was dressed. 'There's only one bus every two hours,' he reminded her. 'If you don't hurry, we'll miss the next one.'

They ate breakfast alone. Eve was presumably still in bed, but Philippa wasn't sorry to be alone with her son. This intimacy Scott had forced upon her, this sharing of the minutiae of their lives, much as though they were a long-married couple, was something that disturbed her. Sometimes in the morning, responding automatically to his request for another cup of coffee she could almost allow herself to be deceived into thinking they were married. Weakly she allowed her thoughts to drift, caught up in a pleasant world of makebelieve, jerked unpleasantly back to the everyday world when Simon said wistfully, 'I wish my ... Scott was coming with us.'

'Simon....' She saw how truculent he was looking and sighed, stretching out her hand to ruffle the dark hair, so like Scott's in colour and texture, 'Simon, I'm so sorry,' she said it softly, as though unwilling to utter the words. She ought to be reminding him of his own bad behaviour not apologising to him, but deep down inside her was a relentless sense of guilt which would not let her rest. If she could have perceived this day before she had lied to Scott, would she have still taken the same road? She had hurt Simon by lying to Scott, and she had no idea exactly how much damage she had done to her son in her pathetic attempts to save his father.

They caught the bus with ten minutes to spare.

The route to York was a rambling one, through various small Dales villages, and not exactly unpleasant, although Simon chaffed at the length of time it took. 'If we'd gone in Scott's Ferrari, we'd have been there ages ago,' he grumbled, scowling faintly when Philippa gave him a mild rebuke. 'You mustn't call him Scott, Simon.'

'What should I call him then, "Dad"?' He flushed bright red and refused to look at her, adding grumpily, 'Anyway he said I could, call him Scott I mean. He likes me,' he told her.

Did Simon know how guilty he made her feel? Philippa tried to concentrate on the scenery. If only they could get away from Garston she might be able to deal with the problem a little less emotively. Scott must let them leave. She would have to speak to him about it.

She bit her lip remembering how abortive her attempts to do so had proved. She had followed him one morning down to the pool, hoping to have a private word with him when he finished his morning swim, but when he had stood before her, dripping water, his body taut, and sleek, clad only in brief bathing trunks, his proximity had so overwhelmed her that she hadn't been able to say a word.

'What do you want, Philippa?' he had taunted, moving so close to her that she could see the deep sapphire rim close to the pupils of his eyes. 'To continue what Mrs Robinson so inconveniently interrupted the other evening . . .?' She had fled ignominiously then, not looking back, his sardonic laughter scarring her soul.

'Mum, we're here,' Simon said impatiently,

tugging at her arm. 'Come on.' The bus had stopped and she had been so wrapped up in her thoughts she hadn't even noticed.

They spent what was left of the morning exploring the town. Philippa knew it quite well and it hadn't changed, although there was a far better selection of small exclusive boutiques than she remembered.

'Shopping.' Simon pulled a face, 'Do we have to? Can't I go and look at the Minster and then meet you?'

They didn't have an awful lot of time left if they were going to make the three o'clock bus back. Simon was sensible enough not to get lost, and giving him strict instructions where to wait for her Philippa let him go.

She had been in three shops before she found what she was looking for, a soft pink skirt that emphasised her narrow waist and skimmed the slender curves of her hips. She bought a jumper to go with it, Italian knitted silk in multi-coloured pastels, and then on impulse agreed to try on the pretty cotton dress the sales assistant was showing her. Pastel blues and lilacs mingled attractively in a modern design, the dress a simple wrap-over style that was startlingly seductive once she had it on, the cotton fabric emphasising the full curves of her breasts.

'It's rather low-necked,' Philippa protested, when the girl came to see how she was getting on. 'I don't think. . . .'

'Oh, it's not as low as all that. Come outside and see yourself full length in a proper mirror,' the girl suggested. Unwillingly Philippa followed her, coming to an abrupt halt as the boutique door opened inwards and Scott strolled in, followed by Simon. The assistant's eyes flickered over Simon and then Scott, lingering appreciatively on his lean frame and amused eyes, before she directed her attention rather hastily towards Philippa.

'I thought we might find you here.' Scott was studying her with an open appraisal that brought the blood stinging to her cheeks, her eyes throwing angry fire back at him as he smiled at her, the same engaging, heart-stopping grin she remembered from the past and which she had thought had disappeared for ever.

'Thank you, but I don't think I'll bother with this one. . . .' Philippa started to tell the girl, dragging her eyes away from Scott's and anxious only to escape from the shop and discover what he was doing with Simon.

'Oh, but. . . .'

'No, you must buy it. . . .'

Both the girl and Scott spoke at once, 'I like it too, Mum,' Simon told her, 'It makes you look . . . different.'

Rather than argue, Philippa gave in to their combined opposition. The dress was unsuitable for her lifestyle; she would probably never wear it, but just for a moment when Scott looked at her in it, his eyes resting fleetingly on the softly exposed curves of her breasts, she had felt seventeen again, headily in love with someone who loved and wanted her, and for that reason if no other she would buy it.

She had to wait until they were outside to discover what Scott was doing with Simon. He had business in York, he told her noncommittally and had seen Simon waiting for her as he left his accountant's office.

'Simon said you were shopping and I guessed you would be in one of the boutiques along here. It's the best part of the city for dress shops.'

'I suppose it never occurred to you that I might have gone looking for you, Simon,' she scolded her son, trying to ignore her fierce tug of pleasure at having Scott's company.

'If you want to blame someone, then blame me,' Scott interrupted. 'In fact, had I known you intended coming to York I would have offered you a lift.'

How very polite and civilised he sounded, a panther trying to convince its victim he was nothing more dangerous than a domestic cat. Well, she knew differently.

'Simon tells me you haven't had lunch yet.' He didn't wait for her reply, his palm warm against her back as he guided her over a pedestrian crossing. Once the other side of the road had been gained, he added, 'Why don't you both join me? I wasn't looking forward to a solitary meal.'

'Thank you, but no,' Philippa said shortly, trying to ignore the look of resentment on Simon's face, his protesting, 'But, Mum. . . .' brought a warning look to her eyes, but it was too late, Scott had perceived her weakness and leapt at it.

'Oh surely,' he protested, 'you can spare an hour. Simon tells me he's examined the Minster from floor to ceiling. He must be hungry.'

It wasn't fair of him to use Simon against her like this, but wasn't that what he had been doing all along? And yet despite her anger there was a dangerous degree of pleasure in giving way to his urgings, and allowing him to guide them towards a discreetly expensive restaurant tucked away down one of the narrow lanes.

'Ah, Mr Garston, Yes, of course we can find a table for you. Please come this way.'

Scott was obviously well known here, Philippa reflected, trying hard not to be impressed by the decor and luxury of their surroundings. 'Le Jardin' the restaurant was called, and was rather like a huge conservatory with its mirrored walls and profusion of plants. Vines trailed overhead, mingling with the bougainvillaea blossoms, attractive cane furniture, white with patterned green and white cushions, was scattered among the banks of plants, and they were led to one of these tables, discreetly set apart from the others so that they could eat without being overlooked.

Who else had Scott brought here? Cara? At the thought of the American girl a pain like sharp steel knives cut into her heart, her face paling so suddenly that she was conscious of a brief sensation of faintness. She must have swayed slightly because almost instantly she felt the hard grip of Scott's fingers against her arm.

'Something wrong?' he demanded, watching her keenly. He always seemed to be watching her these days in that sharp, far too keen-eyed way of his, as though he was waiting to pounce.

'It's just the heat in here,' she lied. 'I'm all right now.'

He released her with a smile that didn't reach his eyes, and while Simon was sitting down said cruelly, 'Of course, forgive me for jumping to assumptions ... but then I suppose you have learned something in the past eleven years, even if it is only not to repeat your past mistakes.' He was looking at Simon as he spoke and she realised on a fierce stab of pain exactly what he meant.

If they hadn't been in the middle of a crowded restaurant; if Simon hadn't chosen that moment to look up at them, she would surely have hit him, wanting to lash out and hurt as he had hurt her.

Afterwards she couldn't remember what food she ordered, only that it tasted of nothing in her mouth and that she could barely force any of it down. Simon seemed immune to her desperation, talking avidly to Scott. He was hungry for his father's attention Philippa recognised; he seemed to want to store up as much of it as he could. How was he going to react when all this was over; when they were back in London? Giving in to Scott had been a mistake; she should have tried to find some other way to pay for the damage to his car ... but what could she have done?

Against her will she was forced to accept his offer of a lift home, and in vain she protested that she would be quite happy to sit in the back of the Ferrari, leaving the front passenger seat to Simon. She was to sit in the front, Scott insisted, and shakily she did as he bid. The seat belt mechanism refused to respond to her fumbling fingers and Scott, who had been securing his own, leaned forward, brushing away her hands, completing the task for her. As she looked down at his downbent dark head a wave of love so strong that her body pulsed with it washed over her. She wanted to reach out and touch him, to tell him how much she loved him, and her whole body shook with the intensity of her emotions.

Simon was talking to Scott, something about computer-electronics that passed completely over her head and made her marvel at her son's ability to grasp and be excited by such complexities; her talents lay in other directions. She had a flair for languages and literature, although she could remember that she and Scott had always found plenty to talk about. The meal she had just consumed plus the heat of the car combined to lull her into drowsiness so that the male voices became peripheral to her concentration. Her senses relayed to her the smooth play of Scott's muscles as he changed gear; the male scent of him, the unbearable familiarity of his body that tensed hers in tight coils of excitement.

'Wake up, Mum.' With a sense of *déjà vu* Philippa opened her eyes. They were back at Garston Place. How long had she been asleep? Her face flamed as she became aware that the something hard and warm beneath her cheek was Scott's shoulder, and that in her sleep she had curved towards him.

'I'm sorry about that,' she apologised stiffly as she drew away, her movements jerky and uncoordinated, 'Too much wine with my lunch.'

Scott looked at her briefly. His mouth had thinned, his eyes glittering as he watched her. It jolted her to realise how much he must have resented her unguarded intimacy. He was looking at her as though he would like to hurt her. She shivered slightly as she stepped out of the car, her glance falling on an unfamiliar Rolls parked outside the house.

'Looks like we've got visitors. An old friend of yours, unless I'm mistaken. You'd better come and say "hello" to him.'

She was about to protest that his visitors were no concern of hers when she caught the warning note in his voice, and then it was too late to escape. His arm fastened tightly round her shoulders, the pressure of his fingers against the bone physically painful.'

'This way.' He wasn't taking any chances on letting her escape. Simon was at her side, looking slightly perplexed, as Scott thrust open the drawing-room door. Three people were sitting there, Eve, and another couple. Philippa's heart plunged as she recognised Geoff Rivers. 'Quite a surprise.' Scott's voice was heavy with irony and Philippa knew he hadn't missed the sudden tension in her body, but he didn't know its real cause.

Across the room Eve looked at her and Philippa wondered if it was faintly apologetic guilt she read in the older woman's eyes as she greeted their arrival, and said lightly to Geoff. 'Here she is, now do you believe me?'

'Pippa, my dear.'

Scott had released her, leaving her to combat a slightly drunken feeling of being cast adrift without support. It was a frightening feeling, somehow, and she wanted to cling to him for support. Fighting against the sensation she managed to smile at Geoff. He was the only person apart from Sir Nigel who had ever called her Pippa, adopting the nickname in those few short weeks when she had worked for him; a holiday job translating some of the documents he received from foreign companies in connection with the racing stud he ran on his estate.

'Darling, this is Pippa, she worked for me for a few weeks, oh it must be over ten years ago now. . . .'

Scott's dark head inclined towards her as Geoff turned to include his wife in their conversation. 'See how well he remembers you,' he murmured sarcastically. 'It must be ten years ago now,' he mimicked. 'He can't even remember when it was, unlike me . . . I remember exactly how long ago it was, Pippa!'

Philippa remembered Mary Tatlow from the photographs she had seen of her. She had often appeared in the local paper, and Philippa had searched avidly for any small item about her when Jeffrey Garston had told her of his plans. How would she be feeling right now if Mary was being introduced to her as Scott's wife; the mother of his children? She went white and then realised that both Mary and Scott had witnessed her small betrayal, Mary with compassion, Scott with bitter comprehension.

'Of course. How nice to meet you, Philippa. And this must be Simon.' Her smile widened to include him.

'Yes, Eve has been telling us about him,' Geoff put in, his eyes resting thoughtfully for a moment on the downbent dark head.

'I must say he's very cool,' Scott murmured to her, while his mother rang for more tea. 'He didn't bat an eyelid when he was introduced to Simon, but then he must know you've nothing to gain by betraying him. I doubt he would ever tell Mary about Simon—and of course you already knew that he had no intention of marrying you.'

'Seeing as you disapprove so much I'm surprised that you're so indulgent towards my son,' Philippa spat back, infuriated by his arrogant assumptions.

'Ah, but you see, Simon isn't responsible for his fathering, and you are. Besides, I like him. Don't you ever feel guilty for depriving him of a father? Surely there have been applicants for the—er—position over the years?'

'Yes, there have,' Philippa gritted at him, goaded beyond endurance. 'But you see none of them have ever come near comparing with his natural father.'

It was Scott's turn to lose his colour, an ugly fury twisting his facial muscles in an unpleasant mockery of a smile, the muscles in his throat corded with effort. Philippa looked down at his hands and knew that it was only with a very great effort that he was keeping them from tightening round her throat. 'I'm surprised at my mother bringing Geoff here when she knows. . . .'

'That I bore his bastard,' Philippa supplied for him. Inwardly she was shaking with anger, but she wasn't going to let Scott see how much his insults hurt her. 'What's the matter, Scott? Jealous because my child wasn't yours?'

For a second time seemed to be suspended, both of them totally engrossed in one another, the tension between them so tight that it threatened to explode.

'Mine? Dear God, do you think I would allow a

bitch like you to have my child? Once I would
have married you, no matter whose child you
carried; that was how much I . . . loved you. But I
loved a chimera, someone who didn't exist, I loved
a cheating, greedy little bitch. No, I don't wish
you'd had my child, Philippa. In fact I thank God
that I never burdened a child of mine with a
mother like you.'

He turned away from her before she could
speak, going to join the others, leaving her alone
with the waves of pain that threatened to swamp
all her fragile defences. She had thought she knew
pain; that it was something she had come to terms
with, endured; but she had known nothing.
Nothing!

She wanted to leave, to go up to her room and
lock herself away, but she couldn't move. The
voices of the others impinged distantly, like the
sound of the sea against the shore.

'Mum, are you all right?'

She dragged her thoughts together and stared
blindly into Simon's anxious face. Simon! For his
sake she had to pull herself together. 'Fine,' she
assured him. Eve was saying something to her,
proferring a cup of tea, her eyes anxious. She took
it, the cup clattering against the saucer, her nerves
so finely drawn that she wanted to scream to
relieve the tension, and to go on screaming.

'Well, Philippa, it's been lovely seeing you again.
You must come over and see us.' Somehow they
were all standing outside by Geoff's Rolls. 'That
invitation includes you young man,' he added
ruffling Simon's dark hair. Simon shied away,
glowering at him, as though some of Scott's

antagonism towards the other man had rubbed off. 'James will be home from school shortly, you two would probably get along. How old are you?'

When Simon told him, he said, 'Well, James is nine, just a year younger.' She had never told Geoff about Scott, or about Simon, but she could see the way his glance moved assessingly from Scott to his son, before coming to rest on her own pale face. 'Well, if you ever get tired of Scott here, we can always find you a job at Fairmile. . . .'

He climbed into his Rolls and Philippa stood back, tensing as she felt Scott's fingers on her wrist, his breath hot against her ear as he rasped, 'And we all know what your "job" will be don't we, "Pippa"? And you'd go to him, wouldn't you? Wouldn't you?'

He was practically shaking her, where she stood, and she fought to get away from him. 'This can't go on, Scott,' she whispered back. 'You must let me go. Simon. . . .'

'Simon what? Might guess the truth, is that what you're so frightened of?'

'Simon is getting too attached to you,' Philippa told him, breaking off when Eve and Simon turned in their direction. 'We can't talk about it now. . . .'

'So what are you going to do? Come to my room? Are you sure it's talk you want, Philippa, or has seeing him again made you hungry for something only a man can give you? Too bad,' he told her with soft violence. 'I'm not playing stand-in again. You'll just have to want, and I'll enjoy watching you ache.'

On Monday she was back at work, wondering how

she was going to convince Scott that he must let them leave. She heard him on the phone to Sir Nigel when she walked into his office with the post. He indicated to her to leave it on his desk, and then motioned to her to stay.

'Oh yes, I'm sure she's looking forward to seeing you too,' she heard him say, and then the receiver was replaced, his eyes chips of frozen blue in his hard boned face. 'That was your erstwhile employer. He and Sheikh Raschid will arrive on Wednesday.' The phone rang again and Philippa walked back to her own office.

Hank arrived halfway through the morning. 'How did you get on with Cara?' Philippa asked him. He grimaced faintly.

'She's still one very angry lady, but I think I might get there in the end.'

She told him about the Sheikh's visit and he whistled, visibly impressed. 'Umm. That could prove a better contract than Cara's father's. We'll all just have to keep our fingers crossed.' He frowned suddenly, touching light fingers to her cheek. 'You look pale, is. . . .'

Scott's door opened, his voice harsh as he demanded, 'Hank, I want to see you—always supposing you can make time between making out with my secretary. Bring us some coffee,' he ordered Philippa, his tone deliberately demeaning.

Biting down hard on the anger surging up inside her Philippa responded, watching Hank lift his eyebrows behind Scott's back and mouth, 'What's got into him, or shouldn't I ask?'

It was after lunch before she saw either of them again. Hank looked tired, and Scott was scowling.

'Phew, he's in a mood,' Hank commented when Scott disappeared into his office. 'What's biting him? I've never seen him like this before.'

Philippa shook her head. She needed some details from the computer office and asked Hank if he could keep an eye on the phones while she went to get them. When she got back Hank was still lounging by her desk, but the door to Scott's room was open.

'He's calling it a day,' Hank told her, 'said something about going for a swim. My guess is he wants to work off whatever's put him into his mood. *You* wouldn't happen to know anything about that, would you?' His eyes were kind and Philippa felt the tears pricking the backs of her eyes. She tried to blink them back but it was too late and once started she couldn't seem to stop.

'Oh, baby.... C'mon, cry it all out,' Hank ordered her. His shoulder felt reassuringly solid and his embrace was brotherly rather than sexual. 'Want to tell me about it?'

She shook her head, feeling both foolish and embarrassed by her emotionalism.

'I suppose this wouldn't have anything to do with young Simon's rather startling resemblance to a certain person, would it?' Hank pressed softly.

Philippa was just about to reply when she heard the click of the outer door. She froze in Hank's arms, feeling him tense, her body quivering as Scott's ice-cold tones filled the tense silence. 'I'm sorry if I'm intruding, but this does happen to be my office.'

His voice dripped sarcasm, and Philippa longed to be able to turn and face him, but her face was still wet from her tears, and she felt far too vulnerable to expose herself to his probing, lacerating gaze. 'I came back to ask you to check with Mrs Robinson and make sure that rooms will be ready for Sir Nigel and the Sheikh. And, Hank,' Philippa felt the muscles of Hank's arms coil, 'I'd appreciate it if you'd try to restrict your personal activities to your own time.'

Not a word to her, Philippa thought shakily, when the door slammed behind him. Not a single word. 'Sorry about that,' Hank grimaced.

'I shouldn't worry about it.' She sounded tired and dispirited and Hank looked at her enquiringly. 'It's my fault, I shouldn't have given way like that.'

'Umm, if that was a sample of what you've been having to put up with I'm surprised you didn't "give way" sooner.... Want to tell me about it?'

Philippa shook her head, thankful when Hank accepted without trying to push her into confiding in him. It couldn't go on. She had to see Scott; to make him see that for all their sakes he must let her go. He was going for a swim Hank had said, and before she could change her mind, Philippa gathered up all her courage and followed him.

The sound of her approach was muffled by his swift progress through the water. He swam well, a fast overarm crawl that sliced through the water, his back brown and tautly muscled, sleek and firm. Her heart lurched and threatened to stop beating. She waited at the bottom end of the pool, as he came towards her. For a moment she thought he intended to ignore her, but then he stopped, grasping the bar, pushing his wet hair back off his forehead, as he looked up at her.

'What's the matter? Hank not willing to play substitute after all?' he taunted.

'Scott I want to talk to you about Simon. He's . . . he's becoming too attached to you, and you . . .' she made a small noise of mingled anguish and despair in the back of her throat. 'You do nothing to discourage him. I know you want to hurt me and why, but surely not Simon. . . .'

'And he is what you came here to talk to me about is he? Are you sure this wasn't what you came for?' He hauled himself out of the pool, his arms binding her. She just had time to grasp the fact that he was totally nude, his body lithely powerful, silk muscles beneath satin skin, and then his mouth clamped fiercely on her own, the heat and damp of his body seeping through her thin clothes, stealing away her resistance, her senses seduced by the proximity of him.

'Scott!' Somehow she managed to pull free of him, turning blindly towards the door, running towards it when he called after her, panic sending the adrenalin pumping through her veins. Dear God, how could he treat her so contemptuously, using her as though she were some sort of disposable inanimate object? Pain seared every nerve ending, her body quivering with it; with the torment of wanting him, loving him, knowing how easily she could have given way to him, drowning in her need for him, while all he wanted was a moment's physical satisfaction and the pleasure of baiting her.

CHAPTER EIGHT

'WHAT time did Sir Nigel say they would arrive?' Scott glanced automatically at his watch, the brief gesture revealing the dark fine hair of his forearm, making him oddly vulnerable. Philippa knew how concerned he was that all would go well with this visit; how important it could be for the future of his company.

'Four o'clock,' she told him. 'Over an hour yet. You'll like Sir Nigel, he's . . .'

'How do you work that one out? On the premise that we both share a common interest? That we're both ex-lovers of yours?'

She tried not to let him see how much his taunts got to her. 'That isn't true. Sir Nigel was simply my employer.'

'Do you expect me to believe that?' he demanded scornfully. 'You must have telephoned him and asked him to get Sheikh Raschid down here, otherwise why would he be doing this? I suppose you looked upon it as a way of making amends, seeing as it was your son who managed to destroy any chance I had of getting the Laine contract.'

'Not *any* chance, surely,' Philippa rejoined nastily, 'You could always have given Cara what she wanted. . . . Or was marriage too high a price to pay?'

His mouth tightened angrily, 'You . . .'

'What's the matter, Scott? Or don't you like getting back what you're so fond of dishing out? I didn't have anything to do with Sir Nigel telling Sheikh Raschid about your new computer.' How could she explain to him her ex-employer's intrinsic desire to help his fellow man? Sir Nigel was one of the nicest people she had ever met; almost too nice to be the head of a multi-million pound business empire. 'He'd read about your computer long before I ever came to work for you.'

He didn't answer.

'Scott, when are you going to let me go?' she asked despairingly, suddenly tired of fencing with him. 'Simon. . . .'

'I'll let you go just as soon as I can afford to, Philippa. As secretaries go, you come pretty cheap.' She flinched under the hidden barb in his words. 'And if I don't get this contract. . . .'

'But if you do, will you let me go?'

His eyes flickered over her face, reading and assessing it, probing every feature until she felt he could almost see into her most private thoughts. 'Why are you so anxious to leave?' he asked softly. 'After all what more could you ask? Geoff so close at hand. . . .'

'You know why I want to leave. I've already told you. I'm worried about Simon.' She gnawed angrily on her lower lip. 'He's becoming far too attached to you, Scott, and you . . . you don't do anything to discourage him.'

'Meaning that you think I'm actively encouraging him? I like him, Philippa, I feel sorry for him as well. It's plain that he wants and needs a father.'

Her fingers curled into her palms in sudden anguish, 'Who told him who his father is?' He asked the question quickly, catching her off-guard. 'I . . . put his name on Simon's birth certificate and he found it. Simon knows . . . that is, he understands. . . .'

'What? That his mother was just a brief pastime to his father and that he was conceived because of it? Is that what he "knows" and "understands", Philippa?'

Anger flared deep inside her at his scorchingly sarcastic and bitter tone. 'Simon knows that I loved his father,' she told him furiously.

'Yes? And does he "love" him too, even knowing that he abandoned him?'

Tears weren't far away, guilt, fear, resentment and an aching tug of love all mixed up inside her. Scott was so righteously indignant on Simon's behalf, not knowing that Simon's father was himself, or that Simon knew most of the circumstances of his birth and yearned for the love and companionship of his father in spite of knowing them. Pride came to her rescue, overriding all other emotions, unconscious hauteur in the tilt of her head as she said quietly, 'I didn't know until recently that Simon was aware of the identity of his father. Naturally he wants to know about him, and I've answered his questions as honestly as I could. I wouldn't want any child of mine to believe he or she was conceived in anything other than love. Simon understands that had the circumstances been different his father would have been there to share his childhood, and yes, I think he does love him.'

'Well, he didn't evince much "love" the other day when he was here. In fact,' he added shatteringly, 'an uninformed bystander would probably think the boy was fonder of me than Rivers! Is that why you're so anxious to get him away from here, Philippa; because you think your son is more attached to me than he is to his natural father? Doesn't that tell you something? Doesn't that warn you how much you've deprived him of? When you first came here I hated you because of the way you cheated me all those years ago. It never occurred to me that I'd begin to hate you for having another man's child as well. Simon could have been our son, Philippa. . . .'

'And if he had been?' she challenged recklessly, holding her breath, her face pale as his eyes raked her vulnerable features. 'If he had been, then you can rest assured that he would have known the love and security of growing up with both his parents. I've been there remember. I lost my father when I was fifteen and that was bad enough.' The harsh clamour of the telephone put an abrupt end to their conversation, but it left Philippa feeling unsettled and vaguely anxious. Life was becoming far too complicated. She would feel much happier if only she knew that Scott was Simon's father. She had seen the way Eve looked at Simon; the affection she gave him; how long would it be before Scott noticed and perhaps questioned it? And then there was Simon himself, so vulnerable, too emotionally responsive to his father already. With a considerable amount of effort she dragged her thoughts back to her work, trying to blot out all her fears and anxieties.

It was just after four o'clock when Sir Nigel's silver-grey Rolls slid to a halt outside Garston Hall. Sir Nigel got out, dapper as ever, his eyes warming as he looked over Scott's shoulder and saw Philippa hovering decorously in the background.

'Garston! Delighted to meet you at last. I've been following your progress in the *F.T.* for some considerable time. Allow me to introduce you to Raschid. Sheikh Raschid, Scott Garston. And Philippa, come and say "hello" to Raschid, my dear.'

Ignoring the furious look Scott was giving her, Philippa walked forward a little uncertainly to respond to her late employer's warm greeting and greet the Sheikh. Sir Nigel had drawn Scott into a low-toned conversation, both men with their backs towards the Sheikh and Philippa, so that Scott did not witness the warm smile the Sheikh gave her, as he recognised her. 'Ah yes, it is Sir Nigel's charming and beautiful ex-secretary is it not? I noticed his office looked far less decorative without your delightful presence to enhance it.'

Ignoring his outrageous flattery Philippa responded demurely. She liked the Sheikh, and knew that beneath the cloak of flattery and charm, he possessed an extremely keen and shrewd mind.

At Scott's request she showed them to the guest rooms which had been prepared for them, and mentioned the sports facilities available.

'Delightful place he's got here,' Sir Nigel told Philippa as he gazed down into the courtyard from the window of his room. 'Makes me think we ought to move out of London. Find ourselves somewhere in the country. Happy are you up here?' He was too shrewd not to have noticed her slight loss of weight and the faint shadows under her eyes, but Philippa shrugged his concern aside. 'Simon is certainly benefiting from it.'

'Mm. . . . Must say it gave me a shock when you insisted on leaving like that. Thought you were quite happy with us. How is young Simon by the way?'

'He's at school at the moment. He should be back shortly.'

'Mmm. Y'know it's a strange thing, but as soon as I set eyes on young Garston, I couldn't help thinking how like him your Simon is.'

It was too late to hide her shock. Philippa knew that her face was parchment pale, her eyes rounding with distressed pain. 'Sir Nigel, I. . . .'

'No need to say another word,' he assured her. 'Shouldn't have said anything in the first place.'

Philippa knew that her old employer would have let the matter go at that, but she shouldn't allow it to drop without talking to him. 'Scott doesn't know . . . about Simon,' she told him awkwardly. 'I. . . .'

'Shan't say a word my dear, I give you my promise. Care to talk to me about it?'

She outlined the story briefly to him, thinking tiredly that the whole situation was developing along the lines of a farce. If matters continued like this for much longer the only person who wouldn't know he was Simon's father would be Scott himself. Her thoughts were reinforced when Sir Nigel said ruminatively, 'Mmm . . . well, I can see why you don't want to say anything, but shouldn't think you'll be able to keep it a secret for much longer. Plain as the nose on your face that the boy's his. I spotted the resemblance straight off. Garston must be blind.'

'I think it's more a case of seeing only what he wants to see,' Philippa said quietly. 'It would be very embarrassing for us both if the truth were to come out now. Scott would feel a moral responsibility for Simon I know, but no blame can or should attach to him for Simon's illegitimacy. If he had known. . . .'

'Well there's always a job for you with us. If you want to come back, Philippa.' He glanced at his watch. 'I'd better go and see how Raschid is getting on. Will we see you at dinner?'

'I don't know.'

Scott hadn't said anything to her about joining them for dinner, and as his secretary in the ordinary course of events she would not have expected to be included. However, the situation was complicated by the fact that she was living in his home. Hank was joining the party and so was Eve. Perhaps the fact that Scott had said nothing to her about it spoke for itself, she decided. The best thing to do would be to go and see Mrs Robinson and ask if she and Simon could have a light supper either in the kitchen or in her room.

She bumped into Simon as he hurried up the stairs, on her way to her room after seeing Mrs Robinson, his hair tousled, his skin tanned, he looked very different from the pale, almost listless boy who had accompanied her to Garston less than a month ago. His 'Hi, Mum' was cheerfully perfunct, but his carefully nonchalant, 'Seen

Scott?' halted her, her forehead pleating in a worried frown.

'Mr Garston has business guests, Simon,' she told him quietly, 'and please try to remember that you and I are here only because I'm working for him.' He was looking sulkily rebellious and she could almost see the words tumbling from his lips, 'Please, Simon,' she begged, suddenly unutterably weary. 'Why don't. . . .'

She broke off as she saw the pleasure dawning in Simon's eyes, and turned her head just in time to see Scott approaching along the landing. 'Hello, son, how did school go today?'

Lean fingers ruffled Simon's already untidy hair, the glowing face her son turned up towards his father making her insides melt with love and fear. Dear God, could Scott honestly not see that Simon was his? With every bit of casual affection and attention he gave Simon he was making it harder for them both to leave. One half of her mind registered Simon's breathless chatter, the other trying to find a way of resolving her ever-present dilemma.

'No, it's your mother I've come to see,' she heard Scott saying, the words focusing her attention on him. 'It seems that Sheikh Raschid would be very disappointed if you don't join us for dinner. . . .'

'But, but I'm only your secretary. . . .' Why was she insisting on hurting herself like this? What did she want him to say? That he would never willingly choose to include her among his dinner guests?

'So you are,' he agreed in a mocking drawl, 'but

the Sheikh is our honoured guest and a potential customer, so. . . .' He shrugged and Philippa felt her nerves tighten in a tense spiral of mingled pain and despair. Did he expect her simply to acquiesce, knowing how little he wanted her there? Couldn't he see that each small confrontation between them was tearing her apart, or could he see it all too clearly? That suspicion froze the blood in her veins. Would he never forget his apparent craving for revenge?

'I'm sorry but I've already made my arrangements for this evening.' Her voice sounded reassuringly cool and serene, but she was jolted out of her hard-won calm when lean fingers gripped her wrist, making her bones protest painfully.

'Yes, so I understand from Mrs Robinson,' Scott agreed smoothly, letting her know that he knew exactly what her 'arrangements' were. 'But I'm sure on this occasion Simon won't mind eating alone. Will you, Simon?'

Simon would accept any suggestions Scott cared to put to him, and Scott, damn him, knew it, Philippa acknowledged wryly, watching her son shake his head.

'So, I'm glad we've got that sorted out. I'll see you at dinner.' Anyone not knowing them might almost have believed that his voice held undertones of pleasure at the prospect, but Philippa knew better. If only she could persuade him to put aside his bitter resentment of her and to let her go. If she didn't escape from the torment he seemed bent on inflicting upon her soon, she feared she would collapse under the strain of appearing impervious to his cruel taunts. But perhaps that was what he wanted. Perhaps? She mocked herself inwardly. What was the point in trying to hope that somehow the past could be wiped out? She kept on hoping that somehow the new Scott was just a barrier, a protective shield behind which the man she loved still existed. But even if it was would she ever be capable of breaching those defences? Hardly, she acknowledged with wry self-honesty, her eyes on Simon as she watched him walk up the flight of stairs which led to his room, before heading for her own.

It was all very well for Scott to command her to join his guests for dinner, but what on earth was she going to wear? At least all her clothes had arrived—she had a full wardrobe to choose from. The same faint spark of hope which urged her to believe the Scott she loved still existed led her to choose a dress she had bought in the sales some months previously. Made up of several soft layers of swirling chiffon in varying shades of pink from palest blush to deep rose, the elasticated neckline with its puff sleeves could be worn demurely on the shoulders, or more provocatively, off them. The sheer top bloused delicately at the waist before the skirt swayed out in a soft bell, the demureness of the almost 'little girl' style belied by the fact that the dress had no underskirt to it and was designed to be worn with the minimum of underclothes. Even at the height of the fashion for it, Philippa had preferred not to go bra-less, but this particular dress she owned, studying it, had to be worn without anything underneath other than the most minimal briefs. Luckily she had developed a light tan, but even so.... After hesitating for several seconds she pulled the dress off the hanger, telling herself she was going to wear it no matter what Scott might think, and telling herself with fine irony that whatever he did think he was hardly likely to guess the truth—that she was wearing it because she wanted him to see her in it. And what? Desire her? Hadn't she had enough evidence of how he felt about her to know how impossible that was?

After she had showered she perfumed her skin with the expensive bodycream Sir Nigel and Lady Rosemary had given her for Christmas, as part of a gift set of her favourite 'Femme' perfume. The cream soothed her skin, the warmth of her body releasing the delicate scent. The pale pink silk briefs, which had been an extravagence she had since regretted, once on looked decidedly provocative. So much so that she found herself trying to avoid her own reflection in the full-length mirror in her room.

At last she was nearly ready. Unwittingly her eyes were drawn to the slender nakedness of her own body, her skin glowing silkily, wrapped in an invisible but sensual cloak of 'Femme'. Her breasts were round and firm, the darker flesh of her nipples slightly puckered, but hardening perceptibly as though sensing the direction of the thoughts she was as yet, unwilling to admit to.

Against her will she found herself imagining the gentle drift of Scott's hands against her body. Her breasts swelled, her nipples tautly erect. Hot colour glowed in her cheeks, and she grasped her dress hastily, trying to dismiss the treachery of her body. As she did so she glanced at her watch. Seven already! She had to be downstairs for half past, which didn't leave her any time to do her make-up and find another outfit.

Quickly applying foundation and then blusher, she made up her eyes delicately, her normally swift, sure strokes unexpectedly clumsy, so that she had to wipe off the blue khol she had applied and start again. Her eyelashes, naturally dark, needed no mascara, which she hated anyway, her lips only the merest touch of soft pink gloss. She turned towards the bed, gazing apprehensively at her dress, before snatching it up and putting it on. It had no fastening, only a pink satin ribbon which tied in a bow at the waist. Her fingers trembled over the small task, her eyes not daring to lift to her reflection in the mirror. Shoes . . . where were her shoes?

She found them at the back of the wardrobe, soft pink kid sandals she had been able to buy cheaply because she was a small size; a lucky buy as they had been reduced to less than a third of their original price. It couldn't be put off any longer. She turned slowly towards the mirror, studying her reflection shakily.

The chiffon glowed softly against her skin, the effect as delicate as mother-of-pearl. Deliberately she pulled down the elasticated sleeves, revealing the pure soft line of her shoulders. The gauzy pink fabric tantalised as she moved, revealing brief glimpses of her body without being openly suggestive. The discerning onlooker could just about make out the shape of her naked breasts, their pink nipples blending with the softly hued chiffon. She brushed her hair, pinning it up in a soft swathe of curls which revealed the vulnerable curve of her throat, soft tendrils lying against her skin. Twenty-five past seven. She couldn't delay any longer.

She gave her reflection a final inspection. Let Scott disapprove and scowl if he wanted to. It was too late now to change a thing.

She wasn't the first in the drawing room. Eve was already there talking to Sir Nigel. She smiled warmly as Philippa walked in, her eyes admiring the picture the younger woman made.

'Philippa, my dear, you look lovely.'

'Both of you look enchanting,' Sir Nigel corrected gallantly. 'Raschid will be even more determined to carry you off,' he added to Philippa, explaining for Eve's benefit. 'Raschid, I'm afraid, is a very practised flirt, who complained bitterly when he discovered that Philippa was no longer working for me.'

Philippa saw Eve's look and laughed. 'And I am far too sensible to allow myself to become a member of Raschid's doting harem. . . .'

'*A* member of it, cherie?' enquired the subject of their conversation in pained tones, as he followed Philippa into the room. 'You do us both an injustice. Were you to consent to come back to Qu'har with me, you would be the *only* member of it. Ah, Philippa, one thousand and one nights of pleasure would not be enough were you to share them with me. I. . . .'

Philippa was laughing at his extravagances when she became aware of the cold trickle of ice along her spine. Without turning her head to look she knew that Scott had entered the room. 'Ah, I see my host is not pleased that I monopolise his secretary,' Raschid whispered mischeviously, 'Why is that, I wonder?'

'Probably because he doesn't approve of Arabian Sheikhs mingling with the hired help,' Philippa responded flippantly.

'Dressed as you are tonight, who could resist you? This,' he touched the soft filminess of her dress, his fingers just below the curve of her breast very dark against the pale fabric, 'reminds me of the costumes of the harem dancers of old, both concealing and revealing. Promising and withholding.' He laughed when she blushed. 'Ah, such innocence, and so rare in these times, even among my countrywomen. What I would give to see your skin flushed with the pleasures of love, little Philippa, your eyes as dark as the velvet nights of the desert! But I see your august boss approaches and will no doubt wish to talk to me of far more mundane matters.'

Raschid was right. Scott was bearing down purposefully on them. His glance moved insolently over her body, probing its secrets, and unlike Raschid she was sure that Scott considered that her dress was more revealing than concealing. Certainly his dark sapphire gaze seemed to have no trouble in finding the soft feminine shape it cloaked nor in distinguishing where chiffon ended and skin began.

A heavy painful heat filled her body, an awareness of him she was powerless to control and she moved away on legs suddenly turned to boneless unsteady supports, leaving him alone with Raschid, but not managing to escape before he had let her know with the searingly contemptuous look he gave her that he had overheard most of Raschid's conversation. Anger scorched her pale skin. Why did he always have to think the worst of her?

Although the meal Mrs Robinson served them was delicious Philippa couldn't really have said that she enjoyed it. She was too keyed up, too acutely aware of Scott sitting at the head of the table, his dark, bitter glances slicing from Raschid to her at intervals throughout the meal, making her conscious of the fact that he was listening to Raschid's bantering conversation and probably putting a totally false interpretation on it. Philippa knew for a fact that Raschid was deeply in love with one of his own countrywomen and that she was at university in Paris where she intended to get her degree and prove her independence before committing herself to marriage. While Raschid approved of her determination, he also regretted it, as he had told Philippa when they had last met. 'You have a way of coaxing the most wary heart to unburden itself to you, cherie,' he had told her wryly when he had finished. 'And because of that you are deceptively dangerous.'

'Your secrets are safe with me, Raschid,' she had assured him, and he had laughed, she remembered, 'Ah yes, mine are,' he had told her. 'But there will come a day when a man gives not only his secrets and his pain into your keeping, but his heart as well.'

Philippa's mouth twisted bitterly. The only heart she wanted was made of marble, cold, hard and totally unfeeling. And as for unburdening himself to her. That was the last thing Scott would do.

When the meal was over Raschid joined Eve and Sir Nigel on the settee in front of the fire. Eve had asked Philippa if she could attend to the coffee. Her arthritis, although much less painful than it had been, still made such tasks difficult at times. Philippa complied willingly and was just bending towards the tray, when she became aware of Scott behind her. Her nape prickled defensively.

'It seems that Sir Nigel thinks very highly of you,' he murmured sardonically, referring to her ex-boss's lavish praise of her during dinner. 'Is that why you're so keen to leave here? Has he promised you your old job back?'

'You know why I want to leave here, Scott,' she managed tonelessly, concentrating on her task. 'Raschid seemed most impressed with the computer,' she added, trying to change the subject and lighten the tense atmosphere between them.

'Yes. He's already promised us an order.'

'Large enough to replace the one you would have had from Cara's father?'

'Why do you ask?' His mouth twisted derisively, 'Surely you don't expect me to believe you feel guilty because you were instrumental in the company losing it?'

At his words a sharp pang of pain knifed through her. Nothing she could say or do would ever alter his conception of her, and the knowledge reinforced her desire to escape; to leave Garston before the explosive situation between them escalated out of control, hurting Simon as much as it had already hurt her.

'No,' she agreed, lifting her head proudly. A brief glance at the settee showed her that the others were deep in conversation and that for a few seconds at least she and Scott had some degree of privacy. 'You know why I want to leave Garston, Scott. Surely what has happened between us already has proved to you that the past is best left dead? With Raschid's contract your company will be well established—you'll have no further need of a cut-price secretary. Please let me go.'

There was a hint of pleading in her voice, and he reacted to it strangely, his eyes dark with something that flickered on the edges of her subconscious, gone before she could recognise the indefinable emotion she had glimpsed briefly.

'Very well then,' he agreed tersely. 'Once the contract is signed you can go.' His mouth twisted. 'To tell the truth once it is signed we shall be so busy that I won't have time to. . . .'

'Get full value out of the situation you've forced me into?'

'Careful.' The blue eyes darkened instantly. 'You don't want me to change my mind and insist on keeping you, do you?'

Keeping her! He would never know how much she yearned for him to do just that. But she wanted his motivation to be love not hatred; she wanted the impossible she told herself jeeringly as he moved away and she completed her task.

For Philippa the remainder of the evening passed in a daze. Once or twice she was conscious of Scott's eyes resting on her, but whenever she looked up he glanced away before she could read his expression. He had agreed to let her go so easily; far more easily than she had expected. Did that mean his hatred for her was lessening or was it simply that he was growing tired of tormenting her?

'Philippa, are you all right?' Eve was watching her worriedly. Poor Eve, she so desperately wanted the sort of fairytale ending that Philippa knew was impossible. Even though she had admitted to Eve that she still loved Scott, part of her recoiled from his angry bitterness even while she understood it. Nothing could dim or lessen her own love, but it was not enough to pierce the barriers Scott had erected around himself. Had he still been the Scott she had known, she would have been able to tell him the truth—that she was unable to stay because of her love for him, but the Scott he had become would simply use that admission to hurt her. What wouldn't she give to wipe out the past; to wipe the bitter cynicism from Scott's face and to restore to his eyes the look of love and wonder she had once seen there. She was asking for the impossible, she reminded herself bitterly. Scott would never look at her like that again. She had destroyed that look, and it made not the slightest difference that she had acted, mistakenly she now realised, for his protection. He had condemned her.

CHAPTER NINE

'HONESTLY, Scott, I don't know what's the matter with you,' Eve scolded her son. 'You've just said that you've got the contract. Raschid is having all the documents drawn up—such a charming man,' she said in an aside to Philippa, 'he even made *my* heart beat faster, although I noticed you seemed immune to him.'

Philippa knew quite well what Eve was trying to do, and for both their sakes she had to stop it.

'Seemed is probably the operative word,' she said lightly, 'I seriously doubt that there's a woman alive who could remain indifferent to Raschid's persuasive flattery for very long.'

Out of the corner of her eyes she saw Scott's frown deepen. So did Eve. 'I don't know why you aren't more excited about this contract,' she complained to her son. 'You really ought to take Philippa out to celebrate. After all if it hadn't been for her connection with Sir Nigel. . . .'

'That had nothing to do with Scott getting the contract,' Philippa felt bound to point out. 'Sir Nigel knew a great deal about Computex long before I came to work for Scott. He has an eye for up-and-coming business, following their progress is almost a hobby with him.'

'Mother is right.'

Philippa stared up into Scott's shuttered face, wondering what it was about the intimacy of the breakfast table that brought this unignorable ache to her heart. His jaw, newly shaven, enticed her to reach out to touch the smooth skin, so much so that she had to forcibly resist the temptation. Her love for him seemed to increase with every day that passed and she lived in mortal fear of betraying to him how she felt. It would be like setting alight explosives. How he would relish her weakness. . . .

'We *ought* to go out and celebrate,' he continued, watching her. 'After all I owe you something for all the hard work you've put in. Philippa plans to leave us shortly, Mother,' he added without turning his head in Eve's direction, 'so taking her to dinner will also be in the nature of a farewell party.'

No, no, I can't endure it, Philippa screamed silently inside. The words even trembled on her lips, but Scott would surely interpret them as a betraying sigh of weakness. Quelling her strong urge to refuse she forced a shaky smile. 'That's very kind of you.'

'Good, I'll make the arrangements. We'll go out tonight.' He pushed back his chair and stood up, 'Oh, and by the way, why don't you wear that pink thing you had on the other night, it suited you.'

It was only after he had gone that Philippa allowed herself the luxury of examining his last words, as carefully as though they were primed bombs, looking for the insult she felt sure was wrapped up somewhere in the softly spoken words.

'Oh, Philippa, I'm so glad you accepted his invitation.' Eve glowed with anticipation.

'*His* invitation?' Philippa emphasised wryly. 'Eve, it won't do any good. You heard what Scott said. I'll be leaving soon.'

'But you love him.'

'Too much to stay. Surely you can see that? He hates me, Eve, so much that I can almost feel it.'

'He does feel very strongly towards you,' Eve agreed, 'but hate and love can sometimes become so inextricably mingled that we can't even tell which is which ourselves. Remember, Philippa, that according to Scott's reasoning he has every reason to hate and despise you. Add to that the fact that he is still very strongly attracted to you physically, and it's bound to cause something extremely explosive, perhaps almost violently so. I'm not completely blind, you know,' she added calmly, surveying Philippa's flushed face. 'Simon told me about seeing Scott in your room. Remember this, Philippa, Scott wouldn't have been there unless he wanted to be.'

'He sees making love to me as a means of punishing me for preferring Geoff.' Philippa said unevenly.

'Umm. He might have convinced himself and you that that is his motivation, but it doesn't convince me. Give him a chance, Philippa, please,' she begged huskily. 'That's all I'm asking from you. Just lower your barriers enough to give him an opportunity to lower his own.'

Let down her barriers. If she did that she was openly inviting trouble, Philippa told herself and yet as she prepared for their dinner date she found herself unable to repress the tiny quivers of excitement rushing through her veins. She hadn't

felt like this since. . . . Since the summer she and
Scott fell in love. Familiar appetite-suppressing
nerve tremors seized her stomach, her heart
thumping so heavily she could almost believe she
could hear it. The pink dress swirled seductively
round her body, her eyes shining with an
excitement she was finding it difficult to conceal.
What on earth was the matter with her? Surely she
was far too sensible to believe as Eve did that all
that was needed for Scott and herself to live
happily ever after was the right opportunity—the
sort of opportunity Eve believed she had created
by forcing this dinner date on them?

She was ready ahead of time and deliberately
forced herself to wait in her bedroom until her
watch showed seven-thirty.

Scott was waiting for her downstairs looking
rather aloof and unbelievably handsome in his
evening clothes. He didn't say a word as he led her
to the Ferrari, courteously opening her door for
her, his only words as he slid in beside her his cool,
'I see you wore the dress.'

'It's the only suitable one I have.'

She just caught the faint gleam in his eyes as he
put the car in gear and then they were drawing
away from the house, encased in a heavy silence
that frayed her nerve endings and left her bereft of
the ability to make the normal social chit-chat.

Scott took her to a restaurant in York itself,
parking the car outside and then taking her arm as
he pushed open the door. The decor was elegantly
plain but Philippa caught her breath as she saw the
tables, their pink and white colour scheme
complimenting her dress, stifling the sudden shaft

of disappointment that speared her as she wondered if this was why Scott had suggested she wear it. What had she expected? That he had made the request because he had liked her in it?

Surprisingly, once they were sitting down Philippa found herself relaxing a little and it was only when they had finished their first course that she realised that Scott had been deliberately drawing her out, encouraging her to talk, subtly steering the conversation so that it never flagged, stimulating all her appetites, she recognised, shivering a little as she saw the danger of allowing herself to succumb to the lure of encouraging the smile curving his mouth to deepen as she described some of Sir Nigel's more outrageous exploits. Just for a moment she had forgotten all that lay between them and instead had given in to the heady pleasure of stretching her intellect to match his, remembering how it had once been between them, and how their conversation had ranged to cover every conceivable topic, their views sometimes clashing, sometimes matching, and all the time steadily building inside her was a hunger and a need that couldn't be satisfied simply with hearing him talk and seeing him smile. She wanted it all, she acknowledged numbly; she wanted his companionship; his conversation; the compatability they had once known both physically and mentally. She wanted his love.

'Something wrong?'

She stared at him, not realising she had replaced her wine glass after barely touching it to her lips.

'No. . . . No . . . nothing's wrong.'

'So, what will you do when you leave Garston?'

Pain seared her, scorching her skin like a living flame.

'I . . . I don't know. . . .' Quickly she lowered her eyelids, not wanting him to see the weakness she knew she was on the edge of betraying. Was it only days ago that she had yearned to escape from him? And yet now here she was wanting with equal if not greater fervour for him to demand that she stay.

It was late when they left the restaurant. Scott had barely touched his wine, but Philippa had finished hers. That was probably the reason she felt so muzzy, she admitted as she fastened her seat belt. She wasn't used to drinking so much, but she had to admit it had a numbing, indeed almost a pleasurably anaesthetising effect upon her senses, deadening the pain which had been with her all evening.

'We're back.'

Scott's voice jolted her into awareness, and she flushed darkly lifting her head from his shoulder. She remembered an overwhelming urge to close her eyes, but it was galling to think that in giving in to it she had turned to Scott.

'I'm sorry about that,' she apologised as she struggled to sit up. She saw him shrug as he reached across her to open her door. The male scent of him reached out to envelop her making her shiver with reaction. 'Yes, you seem to be making a habit of it, don't you? I'll walk you up to your room. Just to make sure you don't fall asleep again on the way.'

The house was in darkness, completely silent, and she blinked when Scott reached for a switch

illuminating the hall. 'Come on.' His fingers
curled round her arm as he led her to the stairs.
Ignoring the inner voice that warned her that it
would be wiser to disengage herself Philippa
gave in to enjoying the touch of his hand against
her skin, no matter how impersonal it might be.
Outside her room he stopped, opening the door.
Later Philippa wasn't sure why she had suddenly
felt so faint, or swayed so instinctively towards
him. Common sense told her that it was too
much wine and too little food, but a deeper less
easily brushed aside instinct said something else.
Whatever the cause, Scott moved swiftly, sup-
porting her weight as he pushed open the door,
and half carried her inside.

Closing it behind them he studied her in the soft
glow of the lamp he switched on.

'It's nothing,' Philippa murmured weakly. 'Too
much wine I'm afraid. It tends to undermine one's
sense of balance.'

'Along with other things,' Scott agreed softly.
'This . . .' he touched the soft folds of her dress, 'is
an extremely provocative garment and one I'm no
more immune to than any other male. I want you,
Philippa,' he whispered huskily, 'and I'm not even
going to ask myself whether my desire stems from
seeing you in this, or consuming little more than
half a glass of wine. Tonight I'm not going to give
myself any excuses. I want you. . . .'

'I want you too.' The words sounded thick and
unfamiliar on her tongue, and for a second she
couldn't believe she had said them. Scott seemed
unable to believe it too. He simply stood and
stared at her, and suddenly it became imperative

that she make at least some attempt to wipe out
the past, to show him, if she couldn't tell him that
he was the only lover she would ever want and
ever had wanted. She moved slightly towards him,
watching the small muscle pulsing in his jaw.

'Philippa!' Her name sounded harsh, almost
desperate as his arms locked round her. She could
feel the fierce thudding of his heart matching the
impulsive rhythm of her own, and all the promises
she had made to herself were forgotten as she
lifted her face to meet his kiss.

There was hunger and need, and yes, anger too,
in the harsh pressure of his mouth on hers, but
there was also, elusively and willpower-under-
mindingly, a bitter sweet trace of the lover she had
once known, and it seduced her away from all her
intentions of withdrawing from him; of telling him
that she wanted him to leave.

'Philippa. There've been so many times when
I've wanted you like this.'

If she hadn't known better she could have sworn
that it was anguish that thickened his voice,
slurring the words until they were a sensual purr
against her skin, but it wasn't her love that Scott
wanted, and yet even knowing that it was
impossible for her to reject him. Something more
powerful than common sense and pride stirred
inside her, some blind overwhelming emotion that
was a combination of love, and regret, mixed with
a helpless compassion for the agony he must have
endured believing that she hadn't loved him.

Her hands touched his hair, caressing the nape
of his neck, the physical sensation of his skin
beneath her fingers so unexpectedly arousing that

what was left of her resistance seemed to evaporate in the heat of her need.

'The look and the scent of you has been driving me mad all evening,' Scott muttered rawly against her ear, his teeth nipping gently at her lobe, 'and as for that dress. How on earth was I supposed to concentrate on what was on my plate when all I wanted to taste was you?' he demanded thickly, one hand entwining in her hair while the other unerringly found the rounded shape of her breast, caressing it until it seemed to Philippa that the heat he generated in her body would burn through the flimsy fabric, so great was her need to feel the warmth of his skin against hers. His thumb gently probing the aroused outline of her nipple through the soft chiffon, Scott muttered thickly, 'Do you remember that first time, Philippa? How I undressed you? This time I want you to undress for me.'

He looked down into her eyes when she tensed, and Philippa wondered if he could sense the conflict in her. More than anything else in the world she wanted to do what he asked, to tease and tantalise him with her body, but to play that game she needed the security and reassurance of knowing she was loved; only that would give her the self-confidence to do what he asked.

'I can't.' The admission trembled from her lips.

For a moment he seemed to hesitate and she half expected him to thrust her away and leave, but just as she thought he would he said softly, 'Then I'll just have to do it for you, won't I?'

The soft whisper of his voice against the vulnerable curve of her throat aroused tiny shivers of response, her whole body trembling as he undid the satin bow securing her dress with slow, sure fingers. It slid from her shoulders in a soft sighing movement that left her exposed and vulnerable, her involuntarily protective crossing of her arms over her breasts provoking a brief smile and a rapid darkening of his eyes.

'If I didn't know better I could almost pretend that you're still as shy now as you were then.' His fingers curled round her wrists tugging gently until she was forced to uncross her arms, her breasts rising and falling rapidly as she strived to control her unsteady heartbeats.

'Philippa, I want you so much.' The words seemed to be torn from his throat, her wrists released as he ran his hands almost fiercely over her body, touching her as though he had lost the benefit of his sight and was totally dependent on the pads of his fingertips to relay the shape and texture of her to himself.

At his touch Philippa felt something quiver and snap inside her, breaking the seals she had placed on her own sexuality. This was Scott, her lover; the man she had hungered for unceasingly while they had been apart; the man she loved with a depth that left her frightened and vulnerable. She murmured his name dazedly as his hands slid down over her back, pushing past the brief barrier of her panties, biting into the soft flesh of her bottom, compelling her against the hardness of his thighs, leaving her in no doubt as to his arousal.

Her body responded instinctively to the knowledge that he wanted her, her hips rotating rhythmically against him, her hands sliding inside his jacket to the fierce heat of his body, while the love she had tried to deny welled up inside her and drowned out the cerebral warnings which had tried to destroy it.

'Dear God, Philippa, have you any idea what you're doing to me?' The thick slurred words reached her from a distance. 'I want you against me—like this.' Scott groaned, wrenching open his shirt, careless of the damage to buttons and fabric as he pulled her back into his arms, crushing the softness of her breasts against the moist warmth of his chest.

The touch of him against her, the rough abrasion of his chest with its covering of fine dark hair stimulated the aching peaks of her breasts, making her writhe instinctively against him, prolonging and increasing the erotic pressure, mindless with the pleasure of it as she arched her throat to welcome the heat of his mouth against her skin.

'Don't do that.' Scott's thick mutter punctuated her delirium as he lifted his mouth from her throat. He watched her shiver, dreading his rejection, and then as though in answer to the question she hadn't voiced, he said softly, 'Because it makes me want to do this.'

'This' was the heated warmth of his mouth taking the tender taut peak of her breast, and teasing it until she cried out with pleasure, abandoning herself completely to his hands and lips, reaching for him totally unable to stop herself from touching him with a compulsive need which surely must have betrayed her love for him, if he hadn't been equally blind, deaf and dumb to everything but the searing need she could feel pulsing through his body.

There was no thought of protest in her mind when he carried her over to her bed, and kneeling beside her removed her briefs, his mouth skimming lightly across her stomach and then her thighs, his hands shaping, touching, smoothing, until she was completely lost in her desire for him.

His kisses burnt her skin, her own lips hot and dry where she pressed them against his sweat damp flesh, feeling the shudders that convulsed him. Obsessed by the taste and touch of him, the barrier of the clothes he was still wearing registered only as an unwanted bar to the pleasure she was taking in touching and tasting him. Again as though he read her mind Scott helped her to remove them, muttering thick, unsteady encouragements, interspersed with brief kisses, barely able to hide the shudder of pleasure tormenting his muscles when he was finally free of his clothes, urging her to touch with her hands and lips the vibrant maleness of his body, and crying out with pleasure when she did so.

It had never been like this before. Philippa felt she had strayed into new, uncharted territory. Both of them seemed to be enveloped in the same fierce compulsion; a feverish need which each fed in the other; a hunger that went beyond words. She knew what had prompted her own; her love, and she refused to allow herself to think about what had prompted Scott's. A hope she had refused to acknowledge before burst into life inside her. Perhaps this was the way, with her body and her touch, that she could show him the truth, reveal to him her love.

His mouth burned against her throat, making her shiver with heated pleasure, her palms sliding down over his back, her tongue finding and striking the flat male nipples surrounded by the soft darkness of his body hair, her already aroused senses leaping in immediate response to his body's unprotected and open reaction as he gasped something unintelligible which could have been either a protest or a hoarse sound of pleasure.

'Philippa.'

If she hadn't known better that raw groan of need could easily have been interpreted as coming from the throat of a man deeply and almost obsessively in love. Behind their fringe of black lashes his eyes glittered dark and unfathomable, only the restless urgency of his body betraying that he was as little in control as she was herself.

His hand touched her intimately and she yielded to his caress not trying to conceal from him how eagerly she awaited his possession.

'You're so beautiful—even more so than I remembered you. I've dreamed of doing this.' His tongue stroked her nipples tormentingly until her body arched and her fingers tangled in his hair in her efforts to prolong the teasing contact, but Scott was impervious to her mute plea, his mouth moving delicately down over her body until her blood ran liquid fire in her veins and she could do nothing but respond blindly to its incitement, 'and this. . . .' His fingers stroked delicate patterns on her inner thigh and then moved upwards drawing from her a reaction which she thought superceded everything she had experienced before until she felt the touch of his mouth against her so intimately that she tensed with the shock of it until she realised that he didn't intend to stop and the ripples of pleasure she had felt before became a full-grown mill race.

'Scott, please. . . .'

He seemed to recognise her plea for what it was; to know how much she ached for his possession; the completeness of the maleness of him, but her own mind seemed to have lost the ability to think rationally because when the first fierce thrust of his body carried her with him upwards through the star-studded firmament around them, when his mouth captured hers it seemed to Philippa that there was tenderness; almost reverence in its touch, and that surely could not be possible?

The world shattered into a thousand shards of pleasure, her body so langorously replete, her eyes closing as she nestled into Scott's arms and let herself drift into sleep.

When Philippa first opened her eyes, her first feeling was one of drowsy pleasure. Scott lay fast asleep beside her, his dark hair tousled, in sleep his face as relaxed as Simon's, all the harsh lines washed away. Last night when they had made love she had almost been able to persuade herself that. . . . That he loved her? She shook her head over her own folly. Last night had been the result of an aberration Scott would no doubt regret the moment he opened his eyes and found her beside him.

Suddenly she knew that she couldn't endure

watching his eyes open and fill with the cold anger she had come to recognise, rejection tensing his body as he turned away from her. Last night she had come vulnerably close to telling how much she still loved him; how much she would always love him, she acknowledged mentally. She had to leave now before Scott woke; before cold reality could spoil her memories of the previous evening. Moving swiftly but quietly she slid out of bed, not giving into an almost irresistible urge to turn her head and look at the sleeping man. This would be the last time she saw him, this would be her last chance to watch him unobserved. Last night he had seemed almost tender. Perhaps she was wrong to go, perhaps. . . .

Perhaps nothing, she told herself sternly. He had spoken no words of love or regret to her; and that tenderness she had experienced so fleetingly probably owed more to her own imagination than any real emotion on Scott's part.

She dressed quickly, taking care not to disturb the sleeping man. She must go and wake Simon and warn him that they were leaving. Simon. . . . She bit her lip. How would her son react when she told him they were going? She slipped quietly out of her room and padded along the landing to the stairs.

'Philippa.'

The sleep-drugged, warm male voice stopped her abruptly, forcing her to turn even though she didn't want to.

'Where are you going?' Scott was frowning, pushing irritated fingers into his hair, his legs bare beneath the robe he had pulled on.

'To wake Simon up and tell him that we're leaving,' Philippa managed to respond evenly. She couldn't meet his eyes. If she did he was bound to read her feelings there. 'That was the arrangement wasn't it, Scott?' pride impelled her to ask. 'You did agree that we could leave once you had the contract? In fact we ... celebrated my departure last night.'

'Last night.' His voice was harsh. 'And this morning you were going to sneak away without. . . .' He had closed the distance between them and Philippa knew without conscious thought that if he reached out and touched her there was no way she could conceal her love. Instinctively she tensed, arching away from him, forgetting the stairs behind her.

'Philippa.'

Scott's sharp warning came too late. She had already stepped back, the sensation of emptiness under her foot disorientating her, Scott's fingers biting into her arm. She raised her free hand automatically, driven by an emotion more powerful than her fear of falling and in that instant saw Simon poised on the stairs above them, his scowl mirroring Scott's as he ran towards them.

'Let go of my mother, you're hurting her.'

She opened her mouth to tell Simon that he had totally misread the situation, but it was too late. 'I hate you,' he stormed childishly at Scott, who still maintained his grip on her arm. 'I wish I'd never found out that. . . .' Some sixth sense warned Philippa of what was to come. She cried out his name, but it was too late to stop him, and her senses whirled in a mixture of anguish and mortification, Simon's voice shrill where it had been hoarse, as he concluded '. . . you are my father. . . . I hate you . . . I hate you. . . .'

'Simon. . . .' Simon rushed towards her just as Scott released her wrist, his face pale with disbelief, his eyes demanding an answer to the question she knew he was going to ask, but suddenly the landing seemed to move giddily around her. She stepped backwards, forgetting the stairs, and the last thing she remembered was the sound of Simon's voice, frightened and full of pain as he screamed out, 'You've killed my mother. . . .'

'Ah . . . you've come round at last.' Philippa opened her eyes. She had been having the most unpleasant dream, but what was Eve doing in her room? She glanced towards the window and saw that the sun was high, and apprehension trickled coldly down her spine. 'It wasn't a dream was it?' she asked in a low voice. 'I really did fall down the stairs, and Simon. . . .'

Eve avoided her eyes and got up from the chair, moving restlessly around the room. 'I must go and find Scott, dear. He told me to fetch him when you came round. There's nothing wrong. You didn't break anything, but Doctor Forbes thought it best to give you a tranquillising shot. He said he thought you'd had a bad shock, and of course poor Simon was practically hysterical.

'Simon!' She tried to sit up, wincing as her bruised spine protested.

'He's all right now. He's with Scott.'

Scott! Simon had said he hated him!

'I'd better go and get him.'

'No, please. . . .' Philippa reached out to touch the other woman's arm. 'Please, I don't want to see him yet. . . .'

'I'm afraid you don't have much choice.'

She glanced towards the communicating door and tensed as she saw Scott framed in it. He was wearing black jeans and a soft white silk shirt open at the neck. He looked tired and drawn, but his eyes when he looked at her held an implacable purpose that warned her that he was not going to allow her to escape.

'Simon's in the kitchen, Mother, why don't you go down and have lunch with him?'

Philippa thought that Eve gave her a vaguely sympathetic look as she left the room, but her senses were too acutely attuned to Scott for her to be aware of anything else.

He came towards her, pulling up a chair and dropping into it, leaning back, the soft silk of his shirt pulling tautly across his chest.

'Now,' he said softly, 'you and I have some talking to do, and before you start lying to me, Philippa, Simon and Mother have already told me most of it.' He got up and walked over to the window, his back to her, his hands in his pockets, moving restlessly, pacing the floor, suddenly turning to face her, the dark anger in his eyes taking her breath away as he said harshly, 'My son! You deprived me of my son. For God's sake, Philippa, why? You knew I wanted to marry you. You knew that Simon was mine, and yet you deliberately let me think that. . . .' A tiny muscle twitched against his jaw, his body tensing as he moved, and came and sat down again. 'Why?'

'Didn't your mother explain?'

'She gave me some cock-and-bull story about my grandfather telling you he wanted me to marry Mary Tatlow but I can't believe you fell for that. You knew I loved you.'

'You loved Garston as well,' she said quietly. 'I was seventeen, Scott, very deeply in love with you and very naively idealistic. Can't you see?' she said bitterly, 'I wanted what was best for you? I couldn't endure the thought that one day you might regret our marriage; that you might resent the fact that you had to give up Garston for me. I didn't know about Simon then, and then when I did. . . .' she bit her lip. 'You didn't argue when I told you I couldn't marry you. . . . You never tried to persuade me to change my mind.'

'You told me you had another lover, damn you.' He stood up, towering above her, his face dark where it had been pale, his eyes glittering with an intensity of emotion that was mirrored in the high flush of colour along his cheekbones and in the taut rigidity of his muscles. 'And I *did* try to persuade you. I even offered to marry you believing you were carrying someone else's child, if I remember correctly. You weren't the only one who was idealistic and naive.'

Suddenly it hurt to swallow. She didn't want to be reminded of the people they had been. Somewhere along the way they had lost it all; the love; the naiveté; the unselfishness. 'Was he ever your lover?'

He wasn't looking at her, and it could hardly matter now. He had made it more than plain how he thought about her. 'No,' she said tiredly. 'Never

... but it was the only thing I could think of that would make you believe that it was all over between us. ...'

'Effective, certainly. Didn't it ever occur to you though that there might have been a cleaner way? It was like slow poison, making me die slowly, and the only thing that kept me from succumbing completely was my need to survive to show you that you'd chosen the wrong man.'

'It's all a long time ago now.' She felt so tired that all she wanted to do was to close her eyes and sleep. 'Perhaps now you understand why I was so anxious to get Simon away. I had no idea until we came here that he knew the identity of his father.'

'He told me that you said it wasn't my fault that I've never been there for him. He said you told him that he was conceived in love and that he musn't blame me because we weren't married.'

'I didn't want him to think badly of you; to feel that you rejected him.'

'Very gracious of you.' The angry snarl caught her off guard, and she stared up uncomprehendingly into his dark face. 'I hope now you'll understand why he was so ... so jealous of Cara. ...'

'Yes.'

'I think now that the sooner we leave. ...'

'Leave? His voice was dangerously soft. 'Oh, you're not leaving, Philippa, at least not unless you want to leave without my son. Simon and I have had a long talk this morning, once I'd managed to calm his hysterics. He wants to stay here.' He saw the colour drain out of her face and laughed harshly, 'He wants to stay with me, Philippa... '

'But. . . .'

'But what? You'll be very gracious again and allow him to spend part of his holidays with me? Is that what you were going to say?'

He had stolen the words from her lips and she could only stare up at him with growing apprehension. 'Not good enough,' he drawled softly, 'Simon is my son, and I want him with me. My mother wants him too. He is her grandson after all. . . .'

'But you can't do that . . . Simon's place is with me.'

'With both of us.'

Her mouth went dry. 'Scott, I don't know what you're suggesting but. . . .'

'What I'm suggesting is we do what we ought to have done eleven years ago. We're getting married, Philippa, and we're going to give our son the unity of a proper family circle; something I think we both owe him, don't you? We both know what it's like growing up without both parents, so don't try telling me that he's happy. He wants and needs me, Philippa, and he wants and needs you as well.'

'And you're suggesting we get married because of that?'

'Can you think of a better reason?' His voice was taut with barely suppressed exhaustion. 'Don't you think we owe it to him? Don't you think he has the right to a little happiness; a little security? I could fight you for custody in the courts I suppose, but I have no intention of subjecting Simon to the trauma of a court battle between his parents.'

'This morning you didn't even know he existed and now. . . .'

'If I *had* known he existed, we'd never be in this situation now. If I'd known you were carrying my child we'd have been married eleven years ago, no matter what protests you made. Damn you, Philippa, did you honestly believe I'd let my grandfather dictate my life to me? Did you honestly think I would marry someone else when you knew how I felt about you . . .?'

'You've changed so much, Scott.' She shivered. 'I don't think I can marry you, not even for Simon's sake. . . . There's nothing left of the Scott I once loved. . . .'

'There's nothing left of him because you destroyed him,' he said savagely. 'You took my heart and you ripped it apart. Do you think anyone suffers an ordeal like that and remains as they were? You either give up or you get tough. . . .'

'I can't marry you.'

'You can and you will. As a matter of fact, I've already told Sir Nigel of our plans. He most definitely approves.'

He turned his back on her. 'I'm not going to argue with you about it, Philippa, either you marry me and give our son the kind of stable home life he needs and deserves, or I fight you in the courts to take him away from you. I can give him much more than you ever could,' he warned her, 'and he wants to be with me. I'll leave you to think about it.'

'I want to see Simon.'

'He's been upset enough for one day. You can see him later. Doctor Forbes said you had to rest. . . .'

Rest? How could she rest after the bombshell Scott had just dropped. Of all the outcomes she had dreaded should he ever discover about Simon, marriage had been the last to cross her mind. She didn't want to marry him; in many ways he was a stranger to her, and yet he was Simon's father, and it was true that Simon loved and wanted him. It was a dilemma to which there was no easy solution, and she gave in mindlessly to the drug Dr Forbes had given, letting sleep suck her down into a merciful state of limbo.

The next time she opened her eyes it was dusk. Eve was sitting with her again, and she smiled warmly as Philippa opened her eyes. 'You must be hungry. I'll get Mrs Robinson to prepare you a tray.'

'No, please, I . . . I'd like to talk. Scott wants us to get married,' she said abruptly.

'Yes I know. He came to see me this morning after he talked to Simon. He had a terrible shock, Philippa, and he's justifiably angry. . . . I know you acted for what you thought was the best, my dear, but Scott suffered terribly when he thought you'd preferred another man. The discovery that you'd deprived him of his child . . . well. . . .'

'I can't understand why he wants Simon so much. If he'd wanted children he could have married long before now. . . .'

'Perhaps he never met the right person,' Eve said quietly, adding, 'Surely my dear you must have guessed that he would want Simon. . . .'

'To the extent of threatening to take him from me legally if I don't marry him?'

Eve sighed. 'Philippa, my dear, Scott changed

dramatically after you left him and his grandfather disinherited him, and he's been carrying the burden of your rejection for too many years to lay it down lightly now. Oh, I know outwardly he seems to have changed, but inwardly. ... He was in his twenties when he met you, and very immature, you hurt him badly you know. You told me when you came here that you still loved him, surely....' She broke off and looked at Philippa expectantly. 'Simon is my grandson after all, the only grandchild I'm likely to have.'

How could she tell Eve the truth? That her son had changed out of all recognition? That he simply didn't love her any more and that for her—loving him as she did—marriage to him would be the very worst form of torture?

But in the end it was Simon who decided her. His needs, which had to be placed above her own. Her bruises were more painful the day after the accident than they had been when they were caused, and on Dr Forbes' instructions she had to remain in bed. Simon came to see her just after breakfast, looking pale and just a little defiant. Her heart sank when she saw the wary way he was watching her.

'Are you going to get married then?' he asked her without preamble.

'Is that what you want?'

'Yes.' He bent his head and refused to look at her, and then added on an excited burst. 'We could stay here for ever then with Sc ... with Dad. ...'

His cheeks were flushed. 'Oh, Mum, can we? Can we stay?'

What could she do? Scott knew how vulnerable she was where Simon was concerned and he would not hesitate to use that as a weapon against her, but she would have to make it clear to Scott that any marriage between them would be a purely business arrangement and nothing more, there would be no more nights when he took her in his arms and used the mastery of his body to wring from her an admission of how much she wanted him. Not ever, ever again.

CHAPTER TEN

THEY were married a week later. In the end there had been no need for Philippa to advise Scott of her conditions for marrying him. He had informed her that they would retain their separate rooms and that their marriage would be strictly platonic. His cool assumption of the role she had intended for herself still smarted. What had he feared? That she might have read too much into that last evening they had spent together? He had been so withdrawn ever since that it might not have occurred, and only by preserving the utmost distance between them was she going to be able to prevent him from discovering the truth.

Simon was over the moon, attaching himself to Scott at every opportunity he got. The sight of their two dark heads bent over something, Simon listening while Scott talked, pierced her with a sharp loneliness that almost bordered on envy of her son. He and Scott had formed a tight exclusive circle she would never be invited to join.

Eve too was pleased, and had confessed herself glad to hand over the reins of the house to Philippa. Scott had told her that she could change whatever she liked in their wing, and she had already made one or two tentative plans. She had expected to find time weighing heavily on her hands with no job to occupy her, but instead she found her days were easily filled.

For one thing there was the garden, which she was coming to enjoy, and for another Scott had asked her to arrange a series of business lunches, which needed careful menu planning and a good deal of ancillary work. They were asked out to dinner a fortnight after the wedding by Geoff and Mary Rivers, who extended the invitation to include Eve.

She declined, eyeing Philippa with a brief smile. 'You two go alone,' she suggested, 'I'll spend the evening with Simon, he's teaching me to play draughts.'

Philippa heard the door to Scott's room open as she was applying her make-up. Scott gave her a generous allowance and she had been to York shopping for the sort of clothes she would need to wear as his wife and hostess. Even though she had entered the marriage reluctantly, having done so, she was prepared to do all she could to make it successful, in the business sense. They were married and for Simon's sake, they must be seen to get along well together in public at least.

Tonight she was wearing a new Jean Muir dress, in soft lavender with a dropped waistline and soft flowing pleats. It suited her fair colouring, and she was able to disguise the faint shadows under her eyes with a discreet use of cosmetics. She had lost a little weight since their marriage, and frowned over the narrowness of her waist. If she lost any more people might start asking questions. Happy brides tended to grow slightly plump rather than skinny. She was ready when she heard Scott's brief tap on the communicating door. He too had changed and was wearing a dark, formal suit, and a white silk shirt. He looked tired, lines of strain etched into his skin, and it occurred to her that this marriage which was no marriage was perhaps difficult for him as well.

'Ready?'

His eyebrow arched when she nodded her confirmation. 'I thought you might like to wear these.' He handed her a small velvet box, and she opened it slowly, surprise darkening her eyes as she saw the diamond stud earrings inside it. 'I noticed you don't have any, and I thought these would make a suitable gift—I didn't buy you anything when we got married.'

'They're lovely.' Even to her own ears her voice sounded stilted, but surely that wasn't really disappointment and pain she saw in his eyes? He had bought the gift because he thought it was expected of him. As his wife she would be expected to possess a certain amount of jewellery.

They drove in silence to the Rivers house, which Philippa remembered from the time she had worked there. Their hosts greeted them warmly, Geoff producing a magnum of champagne with which he laughingly toasted the newlyweds. 'Of course, we weren't entirely surprised,' he confided over dinner. 'After all it was obvious that Simon was Scott's son.'

Philippa felt herself blush, and was unexpectedly grateful for the warmth of Scott's fingers curling round her own. 'We would have married eleven years ago, if it hadn't been for the interference of my grandfather. . . .'

'Umm. He was a horror wasn't he?' Mary agreed, wrinkling her nose. 'I seem to remember at one time he suggested to Daddy that you and I marry, Scott?'

She said it so teasingly that Philippa knew that Mary had no idea that that marriage was the reason that she and Scott had parted, but she was conscious of Scott's eyes on her heated cheeks and of the warm pressure of his hand on hers. Weak tears stung her eyes. If only. . . . Surely the saddest words in the English language? How often had she told herself there was no going back; that she and Scott weren't the people they had been, and yet for a moment, with the comfort of his hand on hers she had almost believed it was possible to go back, that. . . . What on earth was she thinking? She knew they could not go back. Shaking off her unhappy mood, Philippa tried to concentrate on the dinner-table conversation, but she was not sorry when the evening came to a close and they were able to leave.

Scott did not talk on the return journey, and it was only when they were both inside the large panelled hall that she saw the tired way he rubbed the muscles at the back of his head.

'Tension,' he told her briefly, as she followed the movement. 'I've been worried about the company's lack of orders, but the Qu'har contract is a good one and it will make all the difference. Fancy a nightcap?'

She shook her head. She had no wish to remain with Scott in the intimacy of the library, although it wasn't until she had reached her own room that she stopped to question her fear. He had made it more than clear since their marriage that what had happened between them had been an aberration, springing perhaps, she was inclined to think, from his fierce need to assuage the pain she had once caused him. Now that he knew the truth; that Simon was his child and why she had left him, that need had gone, and with it the fierce desire she had sensed in him the last time they made love.

She had undressed and was just brushing her hair when the communicating door opened. She saw Scott's reflection in her mirror, her eyes widening as she took in the ruffled hair and open shirt. He had discarded his jacket, and looked very dangerous standing in the doorway, propped up against the frame.

'Scott?'

'Don't worry, I haven't come to claim my husbandly privileges,' he said sardonically. 'It's this damned tension. Unless I get rid of it, I'm going to wake up with cramped muscles tomorrow.' He saw her bewilderment and said dryly. 'I was hoping I might be able to persuade you to massage the back of my neck for me. I can't reach it. . . .'

She wanted to refuse. Her mouth had gone dry with apprehension, and as though he read her mind Scott said cynically, 'I'm not asking you to make love to me, Philippa, so you needn't look at me like that.'

'I . . . I. . . .' Her eyes followed his progress to her bed, where he pulled off his shirt, dropping it on the floor, and then lying face downwards on it, obviously taking her co-operation for granted. She wanted to refuse, but if she did what excuse could she give him? That she was frightened to touch him because she loved him?

His request was a perfectly reasonable one, in his eyes at least.

'Turn off the light will you,' he asked as he heard her approach, 'it hurts my eyes.'

She snapped it off, leaving the room bathed only in the glow from the lamp in Scott's room and sat down beside him, tentatively touching the back of his neck. The muscles were rigid beneath her fingers, his skin dry. The body cream she used on her skin was on the bedside table and she opened it, smoothing some on to his nape, suppressing a slight smile as its scent was released, wondering how Scott would feel about wearing her perfume, but it did the trick, softening the tense skin so that she was able to stroke the bunched muscles with her fingertips gradually becoming less aware of his maleness and more concerned with her task. Slowly she felt the tension seep out, and her hands were aching when she bent forward and asked, softly, 'Any better?'

Scott's head rested on his forearms and he turned it towards her, his eyes dark and unfathomable in the half light. 'Mmm. Philippa, why do you hate touching me so much?'

His question caught her off guard and she bent to put the top back on her body lotion, the fair curtain of her hair hiding her expression from him. 'I. . . .'

'Is it because you think you might respond to me the way you did the night before you. . . .'

'No.' The denial seemed to burst from her throat her muscles tensing. 'I don't want to talk about it, Scott.'

'I agree,' he said softly, 'talking would be a

waste of time, especially when there are other ways of communicating.' He turned over before she could move, pulling her down on to the bed beside him, silencing her protests with his mouth, slowly releasing her throbbing lips to run his tongue lightly over their full contours. 'Scott, please don't do this.'

His thumb followed the line of his tongue, making it impossible for her to think, never mind object, his teeth tasting the satiny skin just inside her lower lip, sending hot waves of pleasure flooding through her body.

'Scott, please,' she moaned again, 'Why are you doing this . . .?' She twisted her head desperately, seeking to avoid the persuasion of his mouth, but it moved capriciously over her skin, seeking and finding the vulnerable curve of her ear, tasting the warm flesh of her throat, his voice muffled against her skin as he said softly, 'Simon should have a sister, or a brother, don't you agree. . . .'

'Scott, no!'

'Philippa, yes!' His mouth was no longer teasing, but urgent as it covered hers, plunging her deep into volcanic pleasure, his tongue sliding past the barrier of her teeth, making her forget that she had vowed this would never happen again. Her pulses thudded out their undeniable response to his touch, her body moving against him hungrily defying all her dictates that it should not, her small gasp of pleasure when he pushed aside the thin covering of her robe and found the rounded warmth of her breast, going unchecked.

He made love to her with a finesse that bordered on tenderness, not allowing her to fight her response, overwhelming her with the stroke of his hands and lips until she was clinging mindlessly to him, raking her nails lightly across the taut flesh of his stomach in a torment of need as he teased the pink crests of her breasts. His every touch seemed to incite her to abandon herself completely to him, losing herself in sensations she had tried to banish, stopping only when he felt the inciting movement of her hips against his, his arousal tormentingly obvious, so much so that she couldn't understand at first why he was pushing her away.

'I thought you didn't want me?'

What did he want from her? Total debasement? 'I want you.' She made the admission dully, adding achingly, 'Please, Scott, I want you.' She closed her eyes, feeling the hot, scalding tears burning against her lids as she compounded her own humiliation.

'Why? Why do you want me, Philippa?' His hand cupped her breasts, his thumb stroking lazily against her nipple until she was writhing helplessly in his arms, shuddering with sexual tension, mindless with the ache he was deliberately arousing, helpless to deny her love for him.

'Is it because you still love me?'

'No,' she lied, twisting desperately away from him, but he wouldn't let her go. 'You do,' he insisted thickly, his mouth moving hotly over her skin. 'You love me, Philippa, say it . . . tell me. . . .' His hand cupped her breast, his mouth hotly sweet as it closed over it, his control suddenly breaking as he felt her response. 'Tell me you love me. Say it, say it,' he commanded between the caresses and kisses that burned her skin. 'Say it . . . Philippa,

say it. . . .' She wanted to deny it, but suddenly she
knew she couldn't, and the words fell from her
tongue in a husky litany that brought a torrent of
heated passion flooding through her body, sensitis-
ing every nerve ending, every centimetre of skin so
that Scott's fevered possession of her body
transcended anything she had known before, her
response tearing a hoarse cry of pleasure from his
throat as their bodies moved feverishly together,
finding their own method of communication, the
words Scott had wanted to hear filling the room as
she cried them out in soft ecstasy against his skin.

'Philippa.' She didn't want to open her eyes, but
she knew that Scott knew she was awake. The
room was in darkness. While she had slept Scott
had gone into his own room and switched off the
light, but why had he come back to hers, and
moreover why was he in bed with her?

'Why did you pretend you didn't love me any
longer?'

'I don't.'

'You just said you did,' he reminded her softly.

'How could I love a man who wants to hurt me
the way you do?' she cried out painfully. 'The
Scott I loved would never. . . .' She swallowed
hard, and said, 'I could understand that you were
bitter because you thought I'd lied and cheated,
but you seemed to hate me so violently that I
thought it was hopeless trying to tell you the
truth.' A deep shudder trembled through her body
and she tensed as Scott drew her to him, reacting
immediately to the warmth of his skin against hers
and the soft brush of his fingers over her body.

'I told myself that I did hate you,' he agreed quietly. 'It was the only way I could retain my sanity. I was sick with jealousy; so much so that it corroded my ability to see clearly, distorting my powers of reasoning. I couldn't look at Simon without remembering how it had been between us, and how you had told me that it meant nothing, that it was Geoff Rivers you loved. But that last night we had together after we had been out for dinner. . . . Why were you so desperately anxious to leave that you had to go without a word to me?'

'You were asleep. I wanted to tell Simon. It was what we had agreed . . . that I would leave. That evening you told your mother I was leaving. . . .'

'Why did you let me make love to you that night?'

'I . . .' she floundered desperately looking for an explanation that wouldn't give her away. 'I. . . .'

'You still love me.' Scott supplied for her softly, watching the colour come and go in her face; the betrayal of her eyes. It was only when he exhaled that Philippa realised how tense he had been. 'My mother told me,' he said roughly, 'but I didn't believe her. I couldn't. Philippa, how could you still love me after what I've done to you?' He groaned the words against her throat, 'You ought to hate me.'

'The way you hate me?' The words were husky with a pain she couldn't conceal, but they had to be said.

'The way I tried to hate you,' Scott corrected still watching her, 'I love you, Philippa.'

For a second she thought her heart had stopped beating, and then it started up again, quick jerky thuds that corresponded with her disordered thoughts. Was she imagining things or was this Scott actually telling her that he loved her? 'Why do you think I was so ragingly jealous of any other man who came near you? Why do you think I leapt at the excuse to keep you here, when I should have let you go, finding you a job, forcing you to stay when you had made it plain that you felt nothing for me?'

'You love me? But I didn't know. I. . . .' Her tears had stopped, and he reached towards her, placing his fingers against her soft mouth. 'How could you *not* know?' he groaned huskily, 'I betrayed how I felt every time I came within a yard of you.'

'I thought you were simply trying to torment me, to make me want you physically.' She flushed a little, remembering how he had touched her and how she had responded, knowing that both of them had been blind mentally, although their bodies had sensed the truth.

'Tormenting *you*?' he groaned again. 'Have you any idea of the agony *I* endured, wanting you, having you in my arms, responding to me, so . . . so eagerly and yet not loving me. It was torture. It stripped my pride to the bone and left me aching with pain, savage with the intensity of it. You gave me your body, but I knew all the time that you were holding aloof from me, keeping some part of yourself hidden.' His voice was raw with a pain that found an echo in her own heart.

'I had to,' she said huskily, 'I couldn't let you see that I still loved you.'

'So you let me think that you were sublimating

your physical desire for Geoff, with me. Dear God, when you told me that I could have killed you. . . .'

'I know.'

'Mmm, you definitely drew blood there,' he agreed softly. 'No man likes to be told he's being used simply as a stud. It's apt to have a decidedly cooling effect upon one's ardour. . . .'

'I hadn't noticed.' She said it demurely and was rewarded with the brief warning pressure of his fingers against her waist. 'You were driving me insane. That night after we'd had dinner together I think I went a little crazy. I was determined to make you admit that you wanted *me*, only that wasn't enough. I wanted you to want *only* me, and not just want, but love. When Mother told me that you did, I couldn't believe it. That was when I decided I was going to force you to marry me. Once married I thought it wouldn't take too long to break down the barriers and get you to admit how you felt about me, thus allowing *me* to admit how I felt about you, but I hadn't taken into account how much I'd hurt you.'

'We've both made mistakes. . . .'

'Umm. . . .' She sensed what he was thinking and said hesitantly, 'I *did* think I was doing what was best for you, Scott, I knew how much you loved this place. . . .'

'But never more than you,' he said with a fiercely desperate anger, 'Dear God, when I knew the truth, I couldn't understand how I could have failed you; how you could ever believe that stones and mortar however precious could mean more to me than you did . . . than you still do. I had

thought you guilty of greed; of betrayal ... I'd
told myself you were shallow, worthless, and that
you'd taken me for a fool. When I discovered the
truth I. ... Tell me again that you love me. ...'

'Always.' She said it softly against his mouth,
feeling his body take fire from hers.

'I love you so much.' He groaned the words
against her mouth, his arms tightening possessively
around her. 'You can't know how much. ... All
these years I've dreamed about holding you like
this. About turning back the clock and finding
that it was all a mistake. I should have had more
trust in you. I should have looked below the
surface, but my grandfather had undermined my
self-confidence so much that I never doubted that
you did prefer Geoff to me. Forgive me?' The
words were muffled by the drumbeat of his heart
against her, but they still had the power to dissolve
the last of her doubts, melting them away to
nothing, trust, love, longing, clearly revealed in her
eyes as she lifted her head to look down at him.

'Only if you forgive me,' she responded softly,
opening her arms wide to hold the hard warmth of
him, knowing that later they would talk again but
that now they would bind each other's wounds,
salving them with the physical expression of their
mutual love.

Scott bent his head, his mouth hotly possessive
against hers, this his first kiss to her as her
husband, her love and the father of their child. 'A
new beginning,' he promised softly. 'Tonight we'll
expiate the past and let it die, agreed?'

'Agreed. Love me, Scott,' she begged softly.
'Love me all the ways I've dreamed of you loving

me in all the time we've been apart. . . .'

'It will be my pleasure. . . .'

She laughed softly into his throat, stroking the hard muscles of his back and teased softly, 'Oh? I thought it might be *our* pleasure.'

YOURS FREE
an exciting
Mills & Boon Romance

Spare a few moments to answer the questions
overleaf and we will send you an exciting
Mills & Boon Romance as our
thank you.

**A special request from the Editors
of Mills & Boon Romances.**

We are always striving
to provide you with just the type of
romantic fiction you want to read.

Also, in order to maintain our high standards
of quality, we need to learn from you
whether you enjoyed the book
you have just read.

So please help us to continue to bring you
the very best in romantic fiction
by completing the simple
questionnaire overleaf.

**Don't forget to fill in your name and address
— so we know where to send your FREE BOOK.**

See over →

Just answer these simple questions for your FREE BOOK:

1. What is the title of the Romance you have just read?

_____

Author's Name _____

2. Are you a regular Mills & Boon reader?

Yes ☐   No ☐

(a) If 'No', is this the type of romance you expected?

Yes ☐   No ☐

(b) If 'Yes', is this book up to standard?

Yes ☐   No ☐

3. Is there any particular type of romance you would like to see from Mills & Boon?

_____

4. Which age group are you in?

☐ 16-20,   ☐ 21-30,   ☐ 31-40,   ☐ 41-45,   ☐ 45+

5. What made you buy this book? (tick one only)

(a) the author ☐   (d) the description of the story ☐
(b) the illustration ☐   (e) the publisher's name ☐
(c) the series name ☐

6. Are there any comments you wish to make?

_____

_____

_____

Please post this off today.

Fill in your name and address, put this page in an envelope (you can fold it if you need to) and post today to:-

Mills & Boon Reader Survey. FREEPOST,
P.O. Box 236, Croydon, Surrey. CR9 9EL

NO STAMP
NEEDED

Name _____

Address _____

_____

_____ Postcode _____

EDQ1